Unraveled

By Jaci Burton

The greatest gift is getting what you never thought you wanted.

Mitch Magruder, rich, successful, wildly popular surfer and entrepreneur, is always on the lookout for the next big wave or the next great deal. So when he's home for the holidays, he jumps at the chance to build one of his famous hotels right on the white, sandy, Florida beach where he grew up. The only thing standing in his way is Greta Mason.

Divorced with two children, Greta welcomes the struggle to make ends meet at the ramshackle beachfront motel her father left her. The motel means everything to her, and no amount of money—or hot nights of persuasion—offered by gorgeous, sexy Mitch is going to change her mind. No matter how much his touch unravels her defenses.

For once, Mitch finds he's the one doing the chasing, and Greta's doing more than throwing a monkey wrench into his perfectly orchestrated world. She's making him think about things he's never considered before, things other than the pursuit of money. Things like settling down with the right woman.

Now if only he can convince her he wants more than hot sex, moonlit nights, and her hotel...

Sweet Charity
By Lauren Dane

A bad boy is about to find out just how naughty a good girl can be.

After eight long years of pretending a horrible one-night stand hadn't happened and wondering if it had been her fault, Charity Harris has finally coaxed handsome bad boy and lifelong friend, Gabriel Bettencourt, back into her bed. It's not just good, it's fanfreakingtastic! Trouble is, he's persisting with his story about not wanting a relationship and not being good enough for her even as their friendship blooms into something looking a lot like love.

Gabriel has ached to make Charity his for years, and finally having her in his bed, not just enduring but enjoying his darker urges is more than he'd ever imagined it could be. Despite what she says, he knows she deserves candlelight and roses, not candle wax and ropes. He'll enjoy her while he can and let go when she finds the right man.

Charity knows Gabriel's game and she's not having any of it. A man can like it rough in bed and still be good and kind. He's exactly the kind of man she wants to marry and she will. She loves him and she knows he loves her and she's not taking no for an answer.

So when he runs off "to think" just after Christmas, it's up to her to let him know that good girls can like it dark and rough and bad boys can be good men.

Holiday Heat

A Samhain Publishing, Ltd. publication.

Samhain Publishing, Ltd.
577 Mulberry Street, Suite 1520
Macon, GA 31201
www.samhainpublishing.com

Holiday Heat
Print ISBN: 978-1-60504-316-6
Unraveled Copyright © 2009 by Jaci Burton
Sweet Charity Copyright © 2009 by Lauren Dane

Editing by Angela James
Cover by Natalie Winters

Unraveled, ISBN 978-1-60504-248-0
First Samhain Publishing, Ltd. electronic publication: December 2008
Sweet Charity, ISBN 978-1-60504-273-2
First Samhain Publishing, Ltd. electronic publication: December 2008
First Samhain Publishing, Ltd. print publication: September 2009

Contents

Unraveled

Jaci Burton

Dedication

Huge thanks to Jambrea for the title suggestion!

To all the Writeminded ladies for loving Mitch and demanding his story.

And as always, to Charlie, who's a constant reminder to me about what love really means.

Chapter One

Mitch Magruder didn't hear the word "no" very often, especially in business, and usually never from a woman. So when he heard that Greta Mason had said no to his offer to buy her rundown, dilapidated shack of a fifteen-room motel right on the sands at Ft. Lincoln Beach, Florida, which just so happened to be his hometown, he knew he had only one choice. He'd have to go home for the holidays, and take care of a little business while he was there. Turning down his sales team and an offer on paper was one thing. Turning down the CEO and a friend of her brother, someone she'd known since she was a kid? That might be different.

Besides, he could be damned charming in person. And surely she wouldn't say no to him—not after he offered her enough money to put her two kids in private school and settle herself in a nice beach condo. Hell, he might even buy the condo for her. It was the Christmas season, after all, and he was feeling generous. Especially if he could get her motel out of the way and clear the beach for one of his resorts.

He turned left at the stoplight and headed down to the beach. The waves rolled up against the white sand shore, beckoning to him and making his stomach tighten. One would think at forty-three he'd be well past surfing age, but it seemed like he could never stray too far from the need to grab a board, climb on top of a wave and ride it in, no matter where he was. If there was an ocean, he wanted to be in it.

And hell, why not? He'd worked hard to build Magruder Enterprises into the multimillion-dollar organization it was. Last year he'd divested himself of his sporting goods company, which gave him more free time to concentrate on the resort aspect of his business, and more importantly, more time to play. He had money, he had time, and he enjoyed his life.

Just him and the waves, which greeted him as he pulled into the parking lot of the Crystal Sands Motel.

Oh, man, this location was perfect. The motel sat on the white sand, not more than fifty yards from the water. There was plenty of room east, as well as north and south of the motel to allow for an expansive resort area. Beachfront property, baby.

He stepped out of the car and took a walk down beachside to get a feel for the traffic in the area.

It was pretty remote. Great when he put up the resort. Not so great for a fifteen-room motel. A few families enjoyed the water with their kids, but Greta had nothing else to offer them other than the ocean. No catamaran, no jet ski rentals, though he did see a net for beach volleyball. She was trying, at least, but her resources were obviously limited.

She needed a lot more.

She needed him.

"Excuse me."

He turned around and was gut punched by a stunning woman. Sun-streaked auburn hair pulled back into a high ponytail on top of her head, she impatiently pushed back tendrils that the wind had blown against her face. Her shorts showed off tanned, well-toned legs, her polo shirt fit tight against luscious breasts and curved down around a waist made for a man's hands. Damn. Dark sunglasses hid her eyes. He wanted to see them.

"Hi there."

"Hi yourself. Um, you're parked at my front door. You checking in or just looking at the waves? I mean, you're more than welcome to park and take a walk on the beach, but if you could move your car, I like to keep the front of the motel open for guests who want to check in."

"Your front..." Holy shit. This was Greta? He was never, ever at a loss for words. He'd stood in front of international conglomerates and executive board rooms and spun multimillion-dollar deals without blinking, but for some reason staring down at the gawky adolescent who'd turned into a siren had suddenly made him a tongue tied teenager again. "Yeah, sure. Let me go move my car."

Then she smiled, and his dick took notice. Perfectly even white teeth and those full, kissable lips.

What the fuck was wrong with her ex-husband? This woman was a prize.

"Thanks."

She pivoted on her bare feet and headed back to her motel.

He groaned. Her ass was just as good as the rest of her body. Rounded, touchable. Kissable. He was getting a hard-on. That just didn't happen to men like him who prided themselves on control.

He focused his attention on the sand instead of Greta and made his way around the side of the motel back to his car. Unfortunately, she was waiting right there by the front door.

"I said I'd move it."

"Sorry. We get beach walkers all the time using this place as a parking lot. I have to protect my paying guests."

He took a glance down the parking lot. Yeah, all three paying guests. How did she stay in business? He climbed into his car and moved it to the back of the lot, then came back to her. "You don't recognize me, do you?"

She peeled her sunglasses off, revealing emerald green eyes he remembered all too well. With a frown, she searched his face, then scanned his body quickly before looking up at his eyes again. "No. Should I?"

Okay, so maybe it had been twenty years or so. Still, it wasn't like he'd aged badly. He was in great shape, dammit. He held out his hand. "It's Mitch, Greta. Mitch Magruder."

Her frown remained for a fraction of a second, then her eyes widened. "Mitch? Holy shit." She bypassed the hand he held out and threw herself into his arms, pressing those full breasts against his chest. He wrapped his arms around her and tried really hard not to get an erection. That would be bad for the business he was going to propose to her.

"Oh, my God, Mitch," she said when she pulled back, still holding on to his hands. "I haven't seen you in years. Like twenty years or something. How are you?"

Her smile was infectious. "I'm doing well. And you?"

She shrugged. "I'm managing just fine. What brings you here? Don said your parents retired to Hawaii to be closer to you. I heard you were quite successful. God, I'm so sorry to keep you standing out here in the overhang. Come inside." She let go of one hand, kept holding on to the other and dragged him inside.

"Heath, this is Mitch Magruder," she said, pulling him past the scarred tiny front desk where a young man shot his head up and stared at Mitch, wide eyed.

"Mitch Magruder the famous surfer?" Heath asked as they walked by.

"Yup," Greta said. "The one and only hometown success story. I'm taking him to the house. Handle things, okay?"

"Sure." Heath stood to lean over the counter as they walked down a short hallway and to a door that Greta opened with a key in the lock. She pushed it open and he followed her through.

He thought she'd take him to her office, but this was like a tiny house—really tiny. A small living room, kitchen area with eating area adjacent, and a short hallway that must lead to bedrooms. He turned to her. "You live here?"

She nodded and motioned for him to sit on one of the threadbare cloth sofas. "I have to. I run the motel, so I'm sort of on call twenty-four hours a day."

This place was a box. His hotel suites were bigger than this. And she lived here with two children? Of course, she didn't know that he already knew that.

"So, you live here by yourself?"

She had gone into the kitchen and came back with two glasses of iced tea, handing one off to him before sliding onto the sofa next to him. She pushed her hair off her face and smiled. "No, with my kids."

"You have children?"

Her smile widened. "Two. Jeff is twelve and Zoey is ten."

"So you must have a husband lurking about."

Her smile died. "No. I'm divorced. It's just me and the kids now."

"I'm sorry."

"I'm not. He wasn't good for me and definitely not good for the kids. We're all better off without him."

He felt the pain in every one of her words, in the haunted look on her face. He was never one to surround himself with women who had an ugly past. Most of the ladies on his arm were single. And younger than him. Of course Greta was younger than him, too, but not as young as the women he usually dated.

Not that he was thinking of dating her. Not at all. He was here to buy out her motel.

He took a sip of the tea and smiled. "Sweet tea. I haven't had it in a long time."

"They probably don't make it in Hawaii, do they?"

He laughed. "No, not really. My mom still does, though."

"How are your parents?"

"Loving Hawaii, and retirement. Dad golfs, Mom has a bridge club. They stay busy and travel. They're taking a cruise over the holidays."

"That's great. I always did like your parents. I was so happy you moved them to be closer to you."

"And how's your mom?"

Greta rolled her eyes. "Feisty as ever. Always in my business. She never interferes in Don's life like she does in mine."

"You're her baby girl. That's why."

"Uh huh."

He laid his hand on her arm. "I was sorry to hear about your dad. He was a great guy."

Again, the shadow crossed her face. "Thanks. We all miss him a lot. He was the light and life of the family. Losing him was hard. And even though he's not around anymore, I feel like he's still here watching over me."

"I wanted to come for the funeral but I was in Japan at the time."

She placed her fingers on his knee. "Don't worry about that. Don understood. We all did. The flowers you sent were beautiful. So was the note and the card."

"Is your mom doing okay?"

She nodded. "She's fine. She copes, stays busy—mostly by getting into my business, like I said."

He laughed. "Does she help you here at the motel?"

"Sometimes. But this is my baby. Dad left the place to me in his will. He knew how much I always loved this part of the family business. Don had the fishing business and he's set with that. Me, I was always down here working the motel." She took a glance out the window at the ocean. "Dad built this place from scratch. It's not much, but it's all I have left of him. He loved it, I loved it, and now it's mine."

Oh, shit. Now he was going to have to take a different approach entirely. He hadn't known Greta would attach a sentimental value to the motel. He set his glass of tea on the coffee table. "Did your dad ever talk about doing any...improvements to the place?"

She nodded and put her feet on the table. "Yeah, we talked about it, but we're not exactly a money making enterprise. We break even most years. Enough to pay the bills. With the house being attached to the property, I can live here and make enough to see to the upkeep of the facility. That's about it. There's never really enough to do much in the way of upgrades. I have ideas, though, so maybe someday."

Then her eyes widened and she turned to him.

"Hey, you're a bigwig in the hotel business."

Come on, Greta, make the connection. Ask me to buy you out. Make this easy on both of us.

"Maybe you could give me some pointers on inexpensive ways I could freshen this place up, make it more exciting and attractive. I really need to bring in more visitors."

Not exactly the opening he was looking for, but he'd take it. "Well, now that you mentioned it..."

She leaned forward, her eyes glittering. "Yeah?"

"I have an idea that I think will really excite you."

She wriggled on the sofa. "Come on, tell me."

He took her hands in his. "Greta, Magruder Enterprises

would like to buy the Crystal Sands Motel property. Our intention is to build a resort right here on this spot."

She looked at him for a moment, then her smile died. She jerked her hands away from his and leaped off the sofa, her bright eyes narrowing in anger.

"Are you out of your goddamned mind?"

Chapter Two

Greta stared down at Mitch, who she'd been so excited to find at her motel. Now she wanted him gone. He represented everything she hated. Big business, those corporate jocks who thought just because they could build monster hotels they could raze her beloved family business like it was nothing. Like it meant nothing.

It was everything to her, to her children, to their future.

It was all she had left of her father. Didn't Mitch understand that?

"I'm sorry, Greta. I thought this would make you happy."

He was so gorgeous. Seeing him again had made her stomach do flip flops. She had been madly in love with him when she was twelve years old in the way that only a first crush could make a girl's toes curl. He'd been nineteen, a beautiful boy with dark hair and a surfer's lean body. He'd taught her to surf, to love the ocean waves as much as he had. He'd taught her all about having a dream and going for it.

She'd had a dream once. Until one man had killed all her dreams.

Never again would she allow that to happen. No man was going to take away her dreams.

"That's why you're here, isn't it? That's why you came back to Ft. Lincoln Beach? When I received that offer on the motel from some…" She waved her hand in the air… "Some joint venture capital group or something, I didn't make the connection."

"They're my investment group, a subsidiary of Magruder Enterprises."

"Whatever. It's all big business and big money to me. So you thought you could come here and sweet talk me in person, that because our families were tight and had a history together that I'd be eager to offload this old run down piece of shit motel, take the money and run?"

She watched his gaze wander around her little house and knew what he saw—the dismal pea green shag carpeting, the blinds that didn't quite center on the windows, the ancient nineteen-inch television, the mismatched furniture, the house that she had never been embarrassed about—until now.

"Honestly? Yeah. It's an incredible opportunity for you and your children. A solid future for them."

"My children's future looks just fine. They go to a great school. They live right on the beach. They're happy."

He stood. "I'm sure they are. But you could secure their college educations, move them into a bigger, better home, give them everything they could ever dream of. You could make your own dreams come true."

"My dreams are doing just fine. I have my father's motel. I have my children. I don't need more than that."

Mitch blew out a breath. "You did understand the offer my investment group made?"

She rolled her eyes. "I'm not stupid, Mitch. I can do simple math."

His lips lifted. "There was nothing simple about those numbers, Greta."

Now he was being insulting. She went into the kitchen,

grabbed the yellow pad of lined paper and tore off the top sheet that Zoey had scribbled on, then brought out the pad and a pen and handed it to him. "Here."

He took them and looked up at her. "What's this for?"

"You seem to labor under the misassumption that I'm some brainless twit who can't grasp basic accounting. So go ahead and write up the offer again. I'll wait." She crossed her arms and tapped her foot, realizing she was acting childish, but she didn't care. She was pissed.

"I think you already saw the number, Greta." He laid the pad and paper down on the coffee table. "What I don't understand is why you said no."

"I think I already made my reasons clear. I'm perfectly happy with my little motel on the beach."

"The one with three current guests? This is prime vacation time, right before Christmas. You should be full."

Damn him. "I have three more reservations for the weekend."

"You barely make enough revenue to get by."

"I do just fine. I don't need your money."

"So you're denying your children a comfortable future, and incredible growth for your town? Why, Greta?"

Last straw. "Get out, Mitch."

"Let's talk about this. I can lay out options, show you—"

"I'm not interested in what you have to show me. You need to leave. I have to get back to work." She moved to the front door and opened it, then waited at the entry until he moved toward it.

"We'll talk again."

She shook her head. "No, we won't."

He walked out and she shut the door, leaned her back against it and exhaled, realizing her hands were shaking.

She was right about this. Dad loved this place. She loved it, too.

Destroying it would destroy her, her memories of him. The kids loved it, too.

Dammit, she was right in holding on to it.

It was all she had left and no one was going to take it away from her.

Okay, that went well.

Mitch stared at the little motel from his vantage point on the hill overlooking the ocean. What a beautiful view this would make from a penthouse suite.

Good thing he wasn't the type to give up easily.

Greta was holding on to the past, on to memories.

Once he convinced her to see reason, she'd sell.

He just needed some allies in his corner. And he knew just where to go for those. Then he'd do a little sweet talking, maybe some wining and dining. She worked too hard, she was myopic, her eye only on the motel. She needed to see what life was like on the other side. Then he could convince her a different kind of lifestyle could be hers, if only she'd sell the motel.

So his original plan to lay out an offer and get her to jump at it might have been off by a few days, but he had some time to kill.

Greta was beautiful. So who better to spend the holidays with than her?

And her family.

Greta had thrown herself into her work the rest of the day, but by the time the night shift came on she needed a break.

The kids had spent the day at her mom's, so she headed

over there to clear her head and eat some home cooking. There were only a few days left until Christmas, and her mom had asked her to come decorate the tree anyway, so she figured this was as good a day as any to throw herself into an activity that would get her mind off Mitch and his irritating offer.

She pulled up into the driveway of her mom and dad's house—despite Dad being gone it would always be their house—immediately noticing the strange car parked at the curb. Don's car was next to hers in the driveway. She'd expected him and Suz to be there for the annual decorating of the tree. Jeff and Zoey would no doubt be in the pool along with Don and Suz's two kids, thirteen-year-old twins Alana and Amanda.

So as usual, decorating night would be a total zoo. Just what she needed to keep her mind occupied.

She threw open the door, immediately assailed by the smell of pine trees, a scent so not indigenous to the central coast of Florida.

"Nice tree," she said, tossing her bag on the table in the foyer. "Don pick that one out?"

Her mother, who always dressed bright and cheerful— today it was khaki capris and a flowered button-down shirt— nodded and looked up at the six-and-a-half-foot giant that nearly filled the small living room. She swept her silvery blond hair behind her ears and turned to Greta with a wide grin. "You bet he did. She's a beauty, isn't she?"

"Uh huh. Where is he?"

"In the kitchen sharing a beer with Mitch. You know he's here for the holidays, don't you?"

Greta's smile died. "Mitch is here?"

"Well, yes. He said he went by the motel to see you today, so I don't know why you're surprised."

"I know he was at the motel, Mom. Why is he here? At our

23

house."

"Because he stopped by to say hello, and since Don was here they had a reunion of sorts, so I invited Mitch to stay for dinner." Her mother came over and grasped her hands. "You look pale, Greta. Is something wrong?" She laid her palm across Greta's forehead. "Hmm, no fever. You do look run down, though. Want me to take a shift at the motel?"

She backed away from her overly concerned mother. "No, I'm fine. Really." She turned and headed toward the kitchen, intent on giving Mitch Magruder a piece of her mind.

She found him sitting at the kitchen table, sharing a beer with her brother, Don, both of them laughing. He glanced up when she entered the room, and her gaze caught an instant flare of heat in his eyes when he looked at her.

Her stomach fluttered and her nipples tightened. She had blown off men's looks and advances ever since Cody, not wanting to invite attention, needing to focus on herself, her motel and her children.

Men didn't interest her—not that way. And after what she'd gone through with Cody, it was easy to be turned off by anything having to do with the male species. But the way Mitch looked at her—reminded her for the first time in a very long time that she was a woman and she hadn't had sex in...God, she couldn't remember when the last time was.

But she wasn't going to have sex with Mitch.

"Why are you here?"

Mitch's lips curled. "Hi, Greta."

"You are so rude, brat." Don stood and gave his little sister a hug.

She tilted her head back and glared at her big brother. "You know what he wants, don't you?"

"Yeah. He wants to have dinner with us. What the hell's the

matter with you?"

Greta's gaze returned to Mitch. "He came to the motel today. His big important company wants to buy the Crystal Sands."

"Yeah, he told me." Don moved back to the table to grab his beer.

"Oh, that," her mother said, coming into the room. "Well, that's up to you, I suppose. Did you make her a nice offer, Mitch?"

"Yes, ma'am, I did."

"Well, I'm glad. Greta, you should think about it. Dinner's almost ready. Don, go tell Suz to drag the kids out of the pool."

That's it? They knew and they weren't pissed? Shocked? Horrified? Throwing him out of the house? What the hell? "Did you hear what I said? He wants me to sell the motel."

Her mother turned to her. "I heard you, Greta. I'm not deaf yet. Now go set the table."

Exasperated, she let out a sound of disgust, grabbed the dishes and stalked into the dining room.

"Your mother threw the utensil basket at me and told me to come and help you."

Her gaze shot to Mitch. "Forks on the left. Knives and spoons on the right." She tried not to slam her mother's dishes onto the table.

"I know where they go, Greta." He followed behind her, laying down silverware after she put down the dishes. "Look, if my being here is going to upset you, I'll leave."

She stopped, inhaled, exhaled, then turned to him. "No, it's fine. Sorry. You can stay."

"Mom! Did you know Mitch was a world-class surfer?"

Greta turned and smiled at her son. "Yes, Jeff. I knew that."

Jeff, her gorgeous, lanky twelve-year-old and budding surfer, clearly had a case of hero worship going on. "He said he'd work with me while he was here for the holidays."

Greta swiveled. "You're staying?"

Mitch shrugged. "Sure. I've got nothing better to do so thought I'd hang out through Christmas."

"Isn't that great, Mom? Oh, and he's going to take a room at the motel, too. Right there on the beach. I can take lessons from him every day now that I'm on holiday break. Isn't that awesome?"

Greta glared at Mitch, who just smiled benignly. "Just awesome, Jeff."

"Me too, Mommy. You said I could learn to surf when I was ten."

She looked down at her golden-haired daughter. "Um..."

"You were about that age when I taught you to surf, if I recall correctly," Mitch reminded her.

"I was not that young."

"Yes you were, brat."

She looked up as Don entered the room, his arm draped around his pixie wife, Suz, who asked with a wide-eyed look, "Mitch was the one who taught you to surf?"

She fell into the nearest chair, defeated. "Yes."

"Cool, Mom," Jeff said. "And now he can teach me."

"And me too," Zoey added.

"It's not every kid who can claim to have learned to ride a board from a world-class surfer. Mitch is famous, ya know."

Greta glared at Don. "Uh, yes, I'm aware of that."

"Can we, Mom?" Jeff asked.

"Yeah, Mommy. Can we please?" Zoey cast her sweet, innocent eyes at Greta.

Mitch grinned. "Guess it's surf lesson time first thing in the morning."

"You aren't going to win this one, brat," Don whispered over her shoulder.

"Apparently not." But she sure hated the triumphant gleam in Mitch's eyes.

"I'll be by later tonight to check in."

She nodded. "I'll call ahead and let Heath know you're coming so he can have your room ready."

"Thanks."

"Dinner's ready," her mother called from the kitchen. "Everyone start carrying things in."

Greta rose and marched into the kitchen, feeling closed in and defeated. She'd come here for family support and they'd all rallied around Mitch instead.

But he still wasn't going to buy her motel, no matter how much her family liked him.

Chapter Three

Mitch spent an uncomfortable night on a lumpy queen-sized bed in a tiny room with a small television, dreaming of the highrise hotel and the three-swimming-pool resort with on-site golf course he was going to build in this spot. That was the only thing that got him through the night. He counted the hours until the gray dawn began to peek over the horizon. Long enough to suffer in the bed. He got up and went in search of coffee.

No restaurant at the hotel. No in-room coffee. He stepped outside and took in a lungful of salty air, closed his eyes and imagined what guests in his resort would see first thing in the morning as they walked out on the balconies of their ocean view suites.

The orange sun lifting above the steely ocean, giving life to the peaceful calm of the sea. Gulls flying overhead looking for an early morning snack. The tangy scent of fresh brewed coffee from either their in-room coffeemakers or room service.

God, he really wanted room service. Instead, he put on his sneakers and took a jog on the beach until he found a restaurant where he could grab a coffee to go. Just the smell of caffeine sent the jolt through his system. He sipped as he took a walk on the sand on his way back to the motel.

Jeff and Zoey were already on the beach behind the motel, Greta standing behind them watching as they played.

She wore board shorts and a white short-sleeved T-shirt that molded to her breasts. Again her hair was pulled back in a ponytail, but the early morning breeze whipped pieces of hair against her cheek. She hadn't seen him yet, her gaze trained on her kids as they played near the surf. Her hands stayed on her hips and she didn't once look away from her frolicking children. She was a good mom—attentive and focused despite the activity around her. She didn't turn away until he was almost next to her, then briefly acknowledged him with a nod.

"Morning," she said, not looking his way.

"You saw me?"

"Of course."

"Great peripheral vision."

Her lips tilted upward. "I'm a mother. I have eyes in the back of my head."

He laughed. "How are their swimming skills?"

"Advanced. No worries."

"Okay." He watched them play with way more energy than most adults had this time of day. "Your kids get up early."

"You have no idea. They're so excited to surf with you today. They were awake before dawn."

"Sorry."

"Don't be. I'm up that early anyway. Besides, you get to play babysitter for a couple hours, saving me from having to drive them over to my mother's early this morning. I owe you."

"It's no problem."

She slanted a glance in his direction. "You say that now. Wait 'til you spend some time with them."

He grinned. "I like kids."

"Spoken by a man who clearly doesn't have any. You have no idea what you're in for."

"I can handle them."

She swept her hands toward the two digging a hole in the sand. "Have at it, then. I'll come check on you in awhile, make sure they haven't buried you."

He let out a snort, turned and walked toward the kids.

"Hey, you two. Ready to surf?"

Jeff leaped to a standing position. "You bet I am. Though I already know how. I'm pretty good at it, too."

"I don't really know how," Zoey said, her hair wavy like her mom's and pulled back in the same kind of ponytail. She had Greta's green eyes too.

"I'll make expert surfers out of both of you. Your mom said you're both great swimmers?"

Zoey nodded. "She taught us when we were babies. Plus we had to take lessons every year."

"She wouldn't let us anywhere near the ocean until she was sure we weren't going to drown," Jeff added with a typical adolescent eye roll that communicated just how uncool he thought his mother was.

"Your mom is smart. Safety always comes first. You'll need to take that seriously or we won't even step foot in the water. Got it?"

Jeff sobered. "Got it."

"Me too," Zoey said.

"Good. Do you have boards?"

"Yeah. They're kind of old, though."

He tousled Jeff's hair. "An old board's the best kind. I'll go get mine, we'll pick up yours, then we'll get started."

They retrieved their boards and climbed into their wetsuits. Not knowing their skill level, Mitch started with the basics. He wanted to be sure they clearly understood safety first. And despite Jeff's protests, he insisted on life jackets for both the kids, even though Greta said they were strong swimmers. He didn't want to have to worry about the kids falling off the boards and drowning. He wanted to concentrate on their surfing skills. Once he was comfortable with their swim skills he'd abandon the lifejackets.

He went over the basics, then they climbed on their boards and went into the water, swimming out past the waves. He had them sit on the boards and stayed behind them to watch, telling them to catch a wave and ride it in so he could test their adeptness. Jeff got up on the first try and rode the wave all the way into shore with no problem. Zoey was a little off balance and fell after a few seconds, but she was a determined little thing. She turned her board around and paddled like a dynamo right back out there and tried it again. And again. The girl never gave up like a lot of kids her age would. And Greta was right, especially about Zoey. These kids were strong swimmers.

Jeff got up every time, had an obvious natural talent, so Mitch worked more with Zoey while keeping one eye on Jeff, who really didn't need to be watched. After working with Zoey and teaching her how to feel for balance, she did better.

And he was having a great time. They were nice kids, polite and exuberant. After a couple hours they took a break and found a snack shack for something to eat and drink under one of the shady tables.

"You're doing great," he said, taking a sip of soda.

"Thanks," Jeff said. "I really like surfing but we don't get to do it much."

"I'm sure your mom is busy and doesn't have a chance to take you out on the waves."

"She does what she can. She used to take us out more before..." Jeff dipped his head down and reached into his bag of chips.

"Before our dad left," Zoey finished, taking a loud slurp

through her straw.

"I'm sorry. That must be hard on you." He didn't want to pry and ask questions about their father.

Jeff shrugged. "He was mean. We don't miss him at all. It's no big deal."

It was a big deal and Mitch knew it. "You have a great mom, though."

"She's really cool," Zoey said. "But she doesn't have a lot of time to do stuff with us anymore. Not like she used to. And even then, Dad never wanted her to play with us. He liked all the attention."

"No, he needed *all* the attention," Jeff finished with a sneer of disgust.

Such grown-up observations from children. And clearly, their father was a dickhead. He'd like to track the guy down and make him suffer for hurting his children that way. Kids shouldn't have to grow up this quickly. Childhood was fleeting enough. He'd had a great childhood, with incredible parents. Security and love had allowed him to dream big and reach for the stars.

Every kid should have the opportunity to achieve their goals.

He could give Greta that for her children. All he had to do was convince her.

"So what do you want to do when you grow up, Jeff?"

Jeff tilted his head toward Mitch. "Not sure yet. I like the water a lot, but not sure I want to be a surfer. Maybe a marine biologist."

Mitch nodded and grinned. "You live in the right place for it."

"Do you know how endangered some of the species in our oceans are, how the effects of global warming are harming the ecosystems of our seas?"

Mitch gaped at Jeff. This kid was twelve. "Uh, yeah, I am aware of that. I'm just kind of shocked that you are."

Jeff laughed. "Just because I surf doesn't mean I'm stupid, Mitch."

Mitch snorted and shoved his shoulder against Jeff's. "Clearly."

"I want to be in the Olympics," Zoey said. "Swimming. I like to swim and Momma says I'm really good at it. But we can't afford the lessons to take me to the next level."

Geez, both these kids were incredible. "Well, you're still young enough, Zoey. There's still time."

She nodded and slurped again from her straw.

After their break they went out in the water again. It wasn't until Greta tracked them down that Mitch realized it was nearly four in the afternoon. They'd only stopped one other time for lunch, and otherwise had spent the entire day playing in the water.

Mitch'd had a great time with the kids. They were fun, attentive, and whip smart. It had been easy to spend the day with them.

Greta tossed towels at the kids. "Time to shower and change. You still have chores to do."

"Okay, Mom," Jeff said, then turned to Mitch and stuck out his hand. "Thanks for the surfing lessons today."

Mitch shook his hand. "You didn't really need them. You're a natural."

His cheeks pinkened. "Thanks."

Zoey threw her arms around Mitch's waist. "I had fun, Mitch. Thank you."

Mitch's heart swelled with an emotion he couldn't name as he hugged her back. "You improved a ton just in one day, miss."

She grinned. "Thanks."

The kids ran off toward the motel, leaving Mitch with Greta.

"You didn't have to spend the entire day with them. An hour would have been plenty."

He turned and walked with her down the beach, letting the sun dry him. "I had fun with your kids today, Greta. They're incredible children."

She tilted her head toward him and smiled. "I think they are. But thank you. I appreciate you giving them some attention. I'd like to give them more."

"You're busy keeping up the motel."

"That's no excuse. They deserve better."

"I can give that to you, you know."

Her smile died. "I don't want to talk about it. I'm not selling the motel to you."

He knew he was pushing it and the timing was off. "Sorry. We won't talk about that." Not right now, anyway.

They walked in silence, side by side, and Mitch had the ridiculous urge to grab her hand and stroll along the sand like lovers.

But they weren't lovers. They weren't dating. They weren't...anything. He had a strong attraction to Greta, but that was physical. Plus, she had something he wanted. That was most likely the lure, and nothing else.

When they returned to the motel, she turned to him. "Again, thank you. I've never seen them so happy. They really enjoyed themselves. I owe you."

"Then have dinner with me tonight."

Her eyes widened. "I...can't."

"Why? Are you working tonight?"

"Well...no. But I have the kids."

"Good. They can come along. You can take me to one of your favorite eating places. It'll be fun."

Fortunately for him, Zoey happened to walk out at just the right moment.

"Can we, Mom? Can we have dinner with Mitch? We can take him to the Galley."

Jeff walked out right behind her. "We're going to the Galley for dinner?"

Mitch grinned. "If your mother says it's okay."

Greta slanted a sideways look at him, as if he'd somehow conspired with her kids against her. This time, he was innocent. But it worked in his general plan. "What do you say, Greta?"

"I guess we're going to the Galley for dinner tonight."

Chapter Four

The Galley was a raucous family-style restaurant located on the Front Pier, surrounded by arcades and shops just footsteps away from the sand and the ocean. The kids loved coming here, mainly for the arcades. Greta hadn't brought them here in at least a year.

Great. Another thing to feel guilty about.

She brushed it aside as the kids dragged Mitch by the hand to a table near the window. They'd gotten there before the rush crowd packed the place in, so they were fortunate to get a spot with a view. Once everyone settled in and ordered their dinner, the kids regaled her with the scoop on their surfing for the day. According to her children, they were practically world-class surfers after one lesson from Mitch.

Mitch sat quietly and listened to the kids boast about their skills.

"That good, are they?"

He nodded. "They did great."

"See, Mom, told ya," Zoey said, lifting her chin. "You know how good I am in the water."

Greta smoothed her hand down her daughter's hair. "Yes, I do."

"You should surf with us tomorrow, Mom."

Greta's eyes widened at Jeff's suggestion, then she shook

her head. "I have a busy day."

Jeff frowned. "You always say that. Can't you take an hour or two off?"

She cast a pleading look toward Mitch, who only smiled. "Yeah, Greta. Surf with us tomorrow."

Damn him. "The motel doesn't run itself, you know." She looked to her kids and smiled. "And my two best helpers are shirking their duties to play in the surf."

Their smiles died on both their faces.

Zoey sniffed. "We can help you, Mommy."

"I'm sorry, Mom. You're right. We'll help you out at the motel instead of surfing," Jeff said.

Shit. That wasn't at all the reaction she'd been going for.

"Oh, no. I've totally got it covered."

"Are you sure, Mom? Because we don't have to surf. We don't want you stuck doing all the work."

Jeff, always the one to worry about her.

"I have a light day tomorrow. So you can help me out in the morning and then surf with Mitch in the afternoon. How's that?"

Jeff nodded. "Okay. That'll work."

How sad that her children worried about her. Was that the role they'd taken on in life? Shouldn't they be allowed to be children? How could she have missed this?

They ate dinner, then she shuffled the kids out to the arcade, insistent that they take at least a little time to be kids. While they played inside the arcade, Mitch led her outside to the pier overlooking the ocean. She could still keep an eye on the kids, but getting outside in the fresh air was nice.

She needed to think, to figure out where she'd gone wrong.

"You're quiet."

She looked over at him. "Am I? Sorry. I'm not very good company."

"I didn't say that. I just said you were quiet. You have something on your mind?"

"No. I'm fine."

"Greta. Something's bothering you."

Now she turned to him. "Really? You know me so well to know that?"

He gave her a half smile. "No. I don't know you at all. But you have revealing body language, and you went quiet during dinner. What started out fun turned...not so fun all of a sudden. Was it something I did?"

"No. Not at all. It was something I did. Something I've been doing. Or not doing. Never mind."

"What do you think you've been doing, or not doing?"

Why was she even talking to him about this? "It's nothing, really."

He swept an errant strand of hair away from her face. "Tell me. I'm a pretty good listener."

"It's the kids. They just seem so...serious. So worried about me."

He let out a soft laugh. "It's obvious they care a great deal about you."

She tilted her head back, looked in his eyes. "They shouldn't care so much. They're kids. I don't want them to worry about me."

"You can't change that."

"Yes, I can. They need more free time to be children. Which means I need to take on more of the work so they can play."

He leaned against the pier railing. "Just what you need— more work to do."

"I can handle it."

He paused, almost as if he wanted to blurt something out. But he didn't.

"What?" she asked.

"If anyone can handle it, you can."

She didn't think that's what he'd originally wanted to say. "Thanks. I do the best I can."

"Don't forget how important it is for you to play, too."

She laughed. "Me? I don't have time to play."

He grabbed her hand. "Sure you do."

He dragged her into the arcade. The kids waved as Mitch pulled her along, stopped at a racing game for two, and shoved her inside. He popped money in the machine, got in next to her and started the game. In no time flat Greta had forgotten all her problems in her zeal to kick Mitch's butt and race across the finish line. She couldn't recall the last time she'd laughed so hard or had so much fun. They played several games. Eventually the kids came over and they took turns switching out partners.

It was a great family night. The kind of night she needed to have more often with her children. And she had Mitch to thank for it.

After a couple hours, Greta rounded up the kids and they headed back to the motel. Jeff and Zoey were both yawning, so she sent them to the house to get ready for bed while she lingered outside with Mitch.

"Thanks for taking us out tonight."

He leaned against her front door, his nearness making her all too aware of how long it had been since she'd been around a man. A very attractive man, too.

"You're welcome."

Damn, he was good looking. Hadn't the man aged at all?

"The kids had a really good time."

He grinned. "I'm glad 'the kids' had a good time."

God, she was really out of practice at this. Not that there was any "this" going on. There wasn't. They'd had a family thing. It wasn't like this had been a date or anything. Still, she felt vibes between them, an awareness that she was a woman and he was a very desirable man. And the way he looked at her told her he felt the same thing. "I had a good time too."

"Good."

She wished she didn't have so many other things on her mind, so much responsibility. It might be nice to ponder that whole man/woman thing with him. She'd had such a huge crush on Mitch when she was a kid.

Some things obviously never changed, because standing out there in the moonlight made her quiver with awareness, with a need she'd thought long ago buried.

He leaned closer. She inhaled, caught the fresh scent of him which only served to remind her how very long it had been since she'd been with a man. And all the reasons she wasn't going to be with one. She couldn't add that kind of a complication to her already very complicated life.

"Well, good night, Mitch. And thanks again."

She slipped inside and grabbed the door. He nodded and smiled.

"'Night, Greta."

Greta closed the door, then exhaled as she leaned against it.

Mitch was a whirlwind, sweeping in with a hurricane force and turning her life upside down. She didn't like it. Not at all. Her life was fine as it was and he'd upset the balance and careful order she'd spent the past few years arranging.

Good thing he wasn't staying long.

Mitch stayed out of sight the next morning, having sensed Greta's tension the night before. He knew she was irritated, but maybe she didn't really know what she was irritated about.

Maybe he didn't really know what she was irritated about, either. It wasn't like he was an expert on women and their emotions. Rich men typically didn't need to be. You threw enough money around and the women he hung out with tended to quiet down.

And didn't that speak volumes about his life?

Good thing he wasn't much into self analyzing. He liked his life just fine. It suited him. No attachments, no emotional entanglements. Fun, sex, travel, the women in his life got exactly what they wanted out of the arrangement, and so did he. No one got hurt. He never made promises he didn't intend to keep. At least he was honest that way.

Greta, on the other hand, was an unknown. She wasn't one of his party girls only out for a good time. He didn't exactly know how to handle her, especially since she hadn't jumped on the chance to take his money.

Everyone wanted his money. Why didn't she? God knows she needed it.

But there was still plenty of time. She'd eventually figure out what he was offering. Then she'd come around.

He waited until after lunch, then put on his wetsuit and found her and the kids. Greta was working on paperwork in the office. The kids were helping Heath.

"Hey," he said, leaning over the counter. "You ready to surf?"

Jeff and Zoey's faces lit up like they'd just been sprung from prison.

"Yes! Is it okay, Mom?" Jeff asked.

Greta looked up from the desk, smoothing away the hair from her face. "Of course. Go ahead."

Mitch was just about to push off from the counter when he paused. "Greta, why don't you come surf with us?"

Her eyes widened, then she frowned and shook her head. "Can't. Busy."

"Aww, come on, Mom." Zoey tugged at her arm.

"Yeah," Jeff added. "Come on. It'll be fun. You haven't been in the water in a long time."

The irritated look she shot Mitch's way spoke volumes. "I have work to do."

"I can do that for you, Ms. Mason," Heath said. "I know how to do it."

Mitch grinned. "See? Problem solved. Go get your wetsuit on, grab your board and we'll meet you on the beach."

She opened her mouth, closed it, opened it again and then looked at the hopeful faces on her kids and sighed. "I guess I can surf for an hour."

"Yay!" Zoey clapped her hands and jumped up and down.

Mitch tried not to laugh. "Come on, kids. Let's head down to the beach."

Fifteen minutes later, Greta joined them at the water's edge, though she didn't look happy about it. Mitch aimed to change that.

The wetsuit clung to her lush curves like a second skin. He liked looking at her. She was a true woman, all soft curves that he'd love to get his hands on.

And that had nothing to do with getting his hands on her motel.

"How long has it been since you surfed?"

She shrugged. "I don't remember."

"Then it's been too long. Come on. Let's get wet."

They got in the water and paddled out to meet the waves to ride them into shore. It may have been awhile since Greta had surfed, but after one or two tries she was up and riding like a pro again. Once a surfer, always a surfer, and she hadn't forgotten the lessons he'd taught her all those years ago. She had awesome balance, rode the board like it was part of her body, and had a great feel for the surf under her.

Soon she was laughing with her kids and having fun, just as he'd hoped she'd do. Her work was all but forgotten as the afternoon slipped by.

They took a break and sat sipping drinks at the snack shack.

"Mom, you're an awesome surfer!"

She beamed under Jeff's declaration and ruffled his still wet hair. "Thanks. Not bad for an old lady."

"I hardly think you're old."

Greta tilted her head back to look at Mitch. "That's because you're way older than me."

Zoey snickered. Jeff snorted.

"Hey, you two," Mitch said. "Watch it."

They laughed louder, then spotted some of their friends and ran down the beach to hang out with them.

"This has been fun, but I need to get back to work."

"Have dinner with me tonight, Greta."

He had no idea why he'd just blurted that out, but chalked it up to part of his plan to woo the motel right out from under her. Deep down, though, he saw the fatigue on her face, the look of utter defeat, and he just wanted to give her something to brighten her up. And that had nothing to do with his plan to buy the motel.

"What?"

"Have dinner with me."

"I...I can't."

"Why not?"

"Because I have work to do."

"You can't always use that as an excuse. You can't work all the time, Greta. We've had a lot of fun with the kids. But when was the last time you had some adult fun?"

Chapter Five

Greta glared at herself in the mirror as she prepared for her date with Mitch tonight.

Correction—she was not having a date with him. They were going out to dinner. Something she should have said no to, but dammit, he'd sucker punched her when she was down and weak. She'd spent the day with him and her children. Her smiling, beautiful children who'd looked at Mitch with something close to adoration in their eyes. They looked at him in a way they had never looked at their own father, quite possibly because their own father had never, ever spent an entire day with his own children. God forbid he should sacrifice his coke habit long enough to even notice he had children, and when he had been around all he'd wanted was for Greta to wait on him hand and foot or to drag her into the bedroom for sex.

She shuddered at the bitter memories, sliding them into the dark recesses of her mind and locking them away.

That part of her life was over. Cody was long gone and forgotten. He'd never disappoint the kids again. He'd never break her heart again. She'd never allow a man to put his needs above hers or her children's ever again.

So why the hell had she allowed Mitch to manipulate her into going out with him tonight?

Because he'd mentioned adult fun. When was the last time she'd had some fun on her own, had something that didn't involve work or her kids?

She couldn't remember. Still, she'd said no, initially.

He'd followed her inside and asked again. In front of the kids. Damn him.

The kids were horrified when she said no, had told her it had been a long time since she'd gone anywhere, and that she was growing—what was it that they'd said—old and moldy, she thought were the exact words—sitting around the motel at night. Jeff had told her she needed to get off her butt and get out, and that he and his sister could go spend the night at Uncle Don's and go fishing in the morning. Then her oh-so-suddenly grown-up son had picked up the phone, called his Uncle Don, and made arrangements to do just that.

Clearly she was not in charge of her own life, or that of her children's. The decision out of her hands, the kids told her she was now free to go out to dinner, and they left to take showers and pack for their overnight visit to their aunt and uncle's. She tried to blame the whole thing on Mitch, but he'd just stood there with a grin on his face.

And now she stood in front of her closet realizing she hadn't gone out on a dinner date with just her and a guy in too long to remember and she had no idea what to wear. Where, exactly, were they going? The fish shack down the beach was capris and a tank top kind of place. The nicer restaurant in town was a sundress kind of place. She'd need to know how to dress. She picked up the phone and dialed his room. He picked up on the first ring.

"Where are we going tonight?"

"Huh?"

"I have no idea what to wear until you tell me which place in town we're eating at."

There was a pause at the other end. "Uhh, hang on."

She waited. And waited. And waited.

"Okay, sorry, Greta. I'll send something over for you in about an hour, okay? Gotta run, my phone is ringing."

"Mitch, what are you talking about. Mitch?"

He wasn't there. Send something over? Send what over? What the hell was he talking about?

Fine. She'd go with the sundress. Better overdressed than under.

She jumped in the shower and was drying her hair when Heath knocked on her door. She opened it to his wide grin and a big box.

"Courier just delivered this."

"For me?"

"Yeah. Said it was from Mr. Magruder." He handed the box over to her.

"Thanks, Heath."

She closed the door, went into her bedroom and set the box on the bed. It was huge, white and unmarked. She pulled the top off the box and gasped. Inside was a shimmery silver cocktail dress along with matching shoes of the same color.

She lifted the dress by its thin spaghetti straps, the whole thing catching the light from her dingy chandelier and shooting sparkling color over her walls.

"Holy shit." He'd ordered this for her? To wear? Tonight? Where the hell were they eating dinner? It looked to be her size. She picked up one of the sexy sandals with the three-inch slender heel. The shoes were the perfect size, too.

Damn, he was good.

She shouldn't. She should be insulted that he would buy her clothes to wear. She should—

Ah, fuck it. He wanted to take her out to dinner, she'd let him. She hurried into the bathroom, did her hair, letting her natural waves do their thing. She left her hair down tonight, just pulled the sides up in a jeweled clip that she found in the nether regions of her makeup drawer. She put on makeup, lip gloss even, then climbed into the dress, which slid onto her body like living silk.

Oh, God, it felt so good, molded against her like it had been created specifically for her curves. She slipped on the shoes and ran back into the bathroom to take a peek.

Damn, she looked good in the dress. She felt like a princess, turned this way and that to watch the dress sparkle. It almost brought tears to her eyes.

You're being silly. Girly. She smiled. She didn't care. She liked how she looked. When was the last time she'd dressed up? Her wedding, probably.

A knock on the door had her running out of the bathroom, smoothing the dress over her hips as she did. Her heart was pounding. She felt foolish getting this excited about something that was just a dinner between...between what? Old friends? They weren't even that.

She opened the door. Mitch had a tux on. Dear God, he looked edible dressed in black and white, his tanned skin looking even more so against the crisp white shirt. He looked impossibly tall and lean as he smiled at her, his eyes raking over her.

"Wow, Greta. You look stunning."

Her face warmed. "I can't believe you sent me this dress."

"I *can* believe you look so beautiful in it." He picked up her hand and kissed her knuckles. She felt it all the way down to her toes, and everywhere in between. Especially everywhere in between. Her nipples tightened and her clit quivered.

"Thank you for this, but there's nowhere in town that we need to get this dressed up for."

He pulled her toward him and slid her arm inside his. "We're not eating in town."

Her gaze shot to his. "We're not? Then where—"

She heard a buzzing sound in the distance, growing louder as if it were headed right for the motel. Mitch walked her out of the house and through the entry as the roar grew louder.

"Wait here," he said. "I don't want your hair to get windblown when it lands."

"You're joking, right?"

He wasn't. The deafening noise landed right in her parking lot, its blades gradually slowing, then stopping.

"Cool, Mrs. Mason!" Heath said, coming around the desk to dash outside.

Speechless, Greta could only stare at Mitch, who smiled at her.

"Ready to have dinner?"

"Where?"

"You'll see."

He took her hand and led her to the helicopter. They'd drawn a small crowd, who gaped at the copter and at them as they moved toward it.

"I've never been in a helicopter." Or on an airplane, or anything that flew. Yet strangely she wasn't nervous at all, just shocked.

"You'll love it." He waited at the door while she climbed in and took her seat, then instructed her how to belt in and put the earphones over her head so they could hear and talk to each other on the ride.

Once they were settled, Mitch communicated to the pilot they were ready to go, and the engine roared to life. Greta grabbed Mitch's hand.

"Don't be nervous. It'll be fine," he said, his voice soothing over the microphone. He slid his thumb over hers, then drew lazy circles over her skin until she was so distracted by his touch she forgot all about being hoisted into the air. All she could do was stare at Mitch, into his incredible eyes, look at his lips, and wonder how this could be happening to her when this morning she'd been in shorts and a T-shirt with sand between her bare toes.

After the first ten minutes or so she relaxed and looked out the window, miles of ocean and sand sweeping by as they flew over it. She had no idea where they were or where they were going, and wasn't sure she cared. This was the experience of a lifetime and she intended to enjoy it, thanks to Mitch.

Thirty minutes later her stomach leaped as they began to descend. She saw lights, lots of them, and the darkness that could only be miles and miles of ocean.

"Where are we, Mitch?"

"Miami."

Her gaze shot to his. "Really?"

The helicopter headed toward a large building right on the beach, but didn't land on the beach, instead hovered over the building, then descended slowly before coming to rest apparently on top of the building. They waited for the blades to stop moving, then unbuckled and Mitch helped her out and toward a doorway where a man dressed in black pants and red coat held the door open for them.

"Evening, Mr. Magruder."

"Hello, Sam."

"Everything is in place as you requested."

"Thank you."

Inside the door was a carpeted hallway that led to a golden-doored elevator. Very ritzy, and obviously a swanky hotel. They rode the elevator down to the main level, which opened onto polished cream marbled flooring. Her heels clacked on the surface as they walked through the lobby, where everyone greeted Mitch with nods and smiles.

"You've been here before?"

His lips lifted in a half smile. "Often."

"You must like the food here."

"It's excellent."

They were stopped halfway down the stairs by a woman dressed in a crisp dark pantsuit. Her nametag said "Paula" and "Manager".

"Oh, Mr. Magruder, we're so happy you're dining with us tonight. Everything has been arranged as you requested."

"Thank you, Paula. As usual, the place looks in tip-top shape."

Paula practically beamed a smile.

Then it hit her as they walked away. She turned to him as they continued their stroll down the stairs and onto a walkway toward the beach. "This is one of your hotels."

"Uh huh."

She paused then, turned around to face the multistory resort with its towering façade overlooking the ocean. It had to have over a thousand rooms, with wide balconies, a swimming pool near the beach, a restaurant poolside, and that was all she had seen so far.

"It's beautiful, Mitch."

"Thanks. I'll give you the grand tour after dinner."

Dinner, apparently, was going to be served on the beach. They took a walk to the right and down a pier, then toward a bungalow, approachable by stepping stones so she didn't get sand in her shoes. A wood overhang and thick drapes closed on three sides so their only view would be of the ocean. Torches were lit outside the tent and the area was closed off by a wall of tall burnished wooden gates on all sides.

Utter privacy. Their own beach.

"Your guests must pay a premium to use this facility."

He led her to the candlelit table and held out a chair for her. "That they do, but many like having a private dinner and a late night swim without having to share the ocean with anyone else. They can even stay the night in here," he said, motioning to the plump sofa with jeweled pillows. "That opens into a bed."

"Seriously?"

"Seriously."

She could well imagine how much fun a couple could have in this cozy little bungalow. Dinner, a swim, then unfold the bed and enjoy some loving magic right there on the beach with the waves crashing against the shore. She shivered.

"You cold?"

"Not at all."

A waiter appeared with a bottle of wine, held it out to Mitch, who nodded and waited while two glasses were filled. Once Mitch tasted and approved the wine, the waiter delivered menus for them. Greta and Mitch both ordered seafood and the waiter disappeared.

Greta took a sip of the wine, then exhaled. "This is wonderful."

"Thank you. My wine stewards do an excellent job selecting only the best wines."

"I think you just like only the best, period."

"I build luxury hotels. My clientele expect a certain level of service, from the rooms to the food to the selection of wines."

"And from the looks of things, they get it. You've done very well for yourself, Mitch. I never would have thought the lanky surfer I knew all those years ago would turn out to be such a connoisseur."

He shrugged. "You can be anything you choose to be, if you set your mind to it."

She took a long swallow of wine. "As long as nothing gets in the way of you achieving your goals."

He nodded. "That happens. You just can't let those drawbacks defeat you."

"Sometimes you have no choice but to settle."

"Sometimes you settle when you don't have to."

She knew he referred to her, to her circumstances, to the motel, but she chose to ignore him. She was going to enjoy her dinner without discussing his offer to buy the Crystal Sands. "How many hotels do you own?"

"Twenty-four in the U.S., twelve abroad."

"Wow. I had no idea."

"We're always looking to expand. Divesting the sporting goods company last year gave me more capital to work with. There are always untapped markets out there prime for expansion or development. A savvy businessperson knows when to capitalize on those markets."

She knew she wasn't going to be able to avoid the topic. "Ft Lincoln Beach, for example."

"Yes. It's a perfect vacation spot with a ton of room for growth. All it needs is a great resort area. You build a super hotel on the beach, suddenly you'll get a water park, great restaurants, and the people will follow. Your town will explode and everyone will benefit."

"And I'm the one standing in the way of everyone's good fortune."

He tipped his glass to his lips and took a sip, then smiled. "I didn't say that."

"You intimated it."

"I didn't invite you to dinner tonight to twist your arm."

"It wouldn't matter if you did. I'm not selling my motel to you, no matter how pretty this dress is."

He laughed. "Good for you. I'd hate to think you were that easy."

Now it was her turn to laugh, and it felt good. She didn't really feel any pressure from Mitch, only from herself. Maybe she *was* standing in the way of progress for her town, but she couldn't help but think he was overexaggerating the growth explosion building one hotel would cause for Ft Lincoln Beach. Sure, it might bring in a little additional revenue for retailers and restaurateurs in town. But an explosion? Unlikely.

Either way, she wasn't selling. Her decision was made. The motel was her legacy from her father. Selling it would be like giving up her memories of him, like insulting his last gift to her. She'd never, ever do that.

They ate dinner—which was incredible—in companionable silence. By the time they were finished eating, the first bottle of wine had been emptied and replaced with another, and Mitch refilled their glasses.

"Are you trying to get me drunk?" She stared at the full goblet.

"Do you get out much?" he replied, deftly avoiding her question.

She snapped her gaze to his. "Me? Uh, no. I never go out."

"Why not?"

She shrugged. "I manage the motel. I have the kids. I'm busy."

"No one should be too busy to have a life, Greta."

"Easy for you to say. You don't have the responsibilities I do."

"Don't I? Granted, I don't have the kids, but my schedule gets pretty full."

"You have...people."

"So do you."

He wasn't making this easy, and she wasn't a whiner. She decided not to say anything at all.

"Your mother could babysit. So can Don and Suz. You're entitled to have a date now and then."

"Yes."

"But you choose not to? Are you punishing yourself?"

She narrowed her gaze. "You don't know anything about me, Mitch."

"I know a little. I'd like to know more. You're divorced, you own and manage a motel virtually by yourself. You have two wonderful kids. Why don't you fill in the gaps for me?"

"There are no gaps. That's pretty much it."

"So why no social life?"

God, he was persistent. "I told you. I'm busy."

"So you're just not interested in men anymore? What did he do to you?"

That one cut a little too close. "I like men just fine. I'm just not interested in jumping on that merry-go-round again. It wasn't fun the first ride."

"Not all men are like your ex."

She sighed. "What did my kids tell you?"

"That he didn't like to spend any time with them, wasn't around much and when he was he liked to monopolize yours."

She stared down at her wine glass. "I really hate that man."

"I do, too. Your children are way too worldly for their age."

She lifted her gaze to his. "And I'm sorry for that. I'm sorry for a lot of things."

"Probably a lot of things that weren't your fault."

"I married him."

"Was he like that when you did?"

"No."

"Then you didn't do it." Mitch leaned back in his chair and sipped his wine. "So what changed him?"

"He had a high pressure job and he hung out with the wrong kind of people who introduced him to the wrong things."

"Like drugs."

She nodded. "He wasn't good at saying no. And he always liked to party. Every weekend. It was part of my attraction to him. He was so full of life and energy."

"That's an attractive quality."

"In the beginning, but not when you're ready to settle down and raise a family. I needed stability at a time when he was least stable. He couldn't handle the responsibility. Drugs and alcohol became his answer. He buckled under the pressure of a mortgage, kids, and the death of my father. I was always the strong one, and I fell apart when my dad died. He couldn't pick up the slack."

"Which meant as he weakened, you had to grow stronger."

"I don't know about that."

"I do. I don't know many women who could handle what you have, Greta. You've done a remarkable job."

How could he say that? She was barely making ends meet. There wasn't a day that went by that she didn't feel like she'd failed her kids.

"Your children adore you."

"They're loyal, and protective."

"They love you. I see it on their faces. But they want more time with you."

Tears stung her eyes. She wasn't going to do this. Not now, not with Mitch. "I give them all I have."

He reached across the table and caressed her cheek. "You're an amazing woman."

She sucked in a breath, refusing to lose it. "Let's talk about something else."

"Okay."

The waiter came and cleared their plates, then brought dessert.

"More food? Are you kidding?"

"You have to try this."

"I can't. I'm so full now."

"Come on. Just a bite." He lifted his spoon and brought it to her lips. She opened her mouth and he slid the chocolate decadence onto her tongue. The ice cream and raspberries burst with flavor on her taste buds.

"Oh, God, that's sinful."

He grinned. "Told you."

Emotional crisis averted, Greta polished off another glass of wine until she finally relaxed, letting all her tensions melt away with every glass of this marvelous liquid. She was surprised when she heard the strains of music from outside the tent.

"Is that a band out there?"

He shook his head. "Piped in through speakers on the building. I don't want my guests' privacy interrupted. Everything within the small compound here is secluded, away from the view of the other hotel guests."

"In case your clients who stay here want to strip off their clothes and go skinny dipping?"

He leaned back in his chair and loosened his tie, casting one very hot look in her direction. "Is that what you'd like to do?"

She couldn't believe she'd said that. "No. Of course not."

He stood and held out his hand. "Come on."

Her throat had gone dry. "What?"

"Stand up."

Jaci Burton

She did. "Mitch, I—"

He pulled her into his arms and her heart did a wild dance. She hadn't been this close to a man since Cody, and that experience hadn't been pleasant. And it had been a long, long time ago. No man had touched her since. She hadn't allowed it, hadn't wanted it.

Until now. She also hadn't opened up to anyone about her and Cody like she had with Mitch. There was something about him that allowed her to feel like she could.

And being with him...well, this was more than pleasant. It made her dizzy, her body coming alive at being so close to a man who looked incredible, smelled so good, wasn't stoned or drunk and smiled at her like she was the most beautiful thing in the world.

So what was wrong with indulging in the fantasy just a little?

A lot was wrong with it. She was a realist. And Mitch was not the kind of guy she should have on her radar. She shouldn't have any man there.

"Mitch, I—" she said again, not knowing how to finish the sentence.

"Shhh, I just want to hold you in my arms and dance with you."

"Dance?"

"Yeah." He tilted his head. "Hear the music?"

She did. Soft, sexy R&B music filtered through the outside speakers. She used to love to dance. Another thing she hadn't done in a very long time.

"Allow yourself to have a good time, Greta. There's no crime in that."

He was right. She placed her hand in his. When he wound his arm around her back and tugged her against him, she realized it had been way too long since she'd been held by a man.

Or had anything else done to her by a man.

She vibrated all over at the thought.

Mitch had beautiful eyes. And his mouth—full lips, white straight teeth. She wanted to kiss him, to feel someone's lips on hers again, to know that exhilarating, heart pounding feeling of desire, to melt in someone's arms until you couldn't breathe.

And when something hard brushed against her hip, her gaze shot to his. He smiled down at her, and her head spun.

Too much wine.

Too much man.

She was in way over her head.

Chapter Six

Greta stood motionless, her feet rooted to the floor of the cabana. Mitch didn't seem to mind, just swayed back and forth, their bodies connected, not asking her for any more than she was willing to give.

Finally, she found her feet and followed him. He led her around the table. The cabana wasn't large, and between the table and chairs and the sofa—correction—bed that loomed in the corner, they had to stay close and dance in small steps. But still, it was magical. The music and the man who held her, the scent of salt breezing in from the ocean, the flicker of torches dancing along the edges of the sand outside, was all a sensual assault that overwhelmed her.

Part of her wanted to fight it, but another part of her realized that was stupid. Mitch was an attractive man, and she was a grown woman who'd had too little fun in her life. He'd offered her an amazing night. She'd be foolish to turn tail and run. He wasn't offering her forever, or even a relationship. As long as she kept her wits about her and realized he was trying to seduce the motel out from under her, she could accept the fun and keep the motel.

She knew exactly what Mitch was up to. But she could still enjoy being with him, without giving him everything he wanted.

"Let's take a walk."

He held her hand while she slipped off her shoes. He took

off his jacket, his shoes and socks, rolled up his sleeves and pants legs, and they stepped out onto the sand. Mitch led her down to the water's edge where the breeze blew stronger, whipping her hair, salt stinging her skin and the waves teasing her toes.

She loved it. This was her home, the water as much a part of her as her own skin. The moon cast a silver glow over the dark water, lending its depths a mysterious quality that had always compelled her.

She stopped and turned to the sea. "I used to stand at the water's edge at night when I was a kid, and could swear all the mermaids and mermen came out in the dark when we couldn't see them."

Mitch slid his hand in hers. "I looked for ghostly pirate ships on foggy nights and imagined stowing away and sailing to the ends of the earth."

She laughed. "The endless dreams of children. How sad that we have to grow up and face reality."

He looked down at her. "Do we?"

"I hardly think there are mermaids or pirate ships out there."

"No, but there are new dreams to believe in. The problem with adults is that so many give up on having dreams."

She turned and started walking again, but Mitch held on to her hand.

"Some dreams aren't attainable," she said.

"You can do anything you set your mind to do."

"Easy if you already have money."

"Not everyone starts with money, Greta. You just have to figure out what you want, then determine how you're going to get it. Then let nothing stand in your way until you do."

"You make it sound so easy."

"Having something that really matters to you is never easy. But it's not impossible."

"Sometimes it is impossible."

He stopped, reached for her shoulders, his fingers warm against her wind-chilled skin. "It's only impossible if you give up your dreams."

"My dreams died a long time ago."

He slid his knuckles against her cheek. "They shouldn't have. You're way too young to give up on what you really want."

"I don't know what I really want anymore. I stopped thinking about myself a long time ago."

"Maybe it's time you started again."

She shook her head. "I don't need or want anything."

His slight smile made her belly quiver. "Don't you? Are you sure there's nothing you want?"

He wasn't talking about her motel. She knew it, and he knew it.

Waves pounded the shore, sending water across her feet. But she stood rooted to the spot, her toes digging into the wet sand as Mitch moved in, erasing any space between them.

Now her own blood rushing through her veins obliterated the sound of the crashing surf. Mitch leaned in and brushed his lips against hers. She tasted wine, the salty spray of the sea, and she raised up, twining her arms around his neck to press closer, hungry for more.

Mitch obliged her, sliding his tongue inside her mouth and licking against hers, then pressing his lips more firmly, tightening his hold on her, bringing her closer to him so she could feel every hard inch of his body. He was well toned for a man his age—hell, for a man way younger than him. His body was all hard muscle as she slid her arms across his shoulders and down his arms. He palmed the small of her back and brought her against the rock hard plane of his chest, his abs, the prominent erection she couldn't—didn't want to—ignore.

Her breathing shallowed as his kiss deepened, and she forgot that his hands were on her ass, that they stood at the water's edge, right there in public. Could someone see them? Did she even care? Her brain was fuzzy—too much wine. She wanted to feel his skin under her fingertips. She had sensory overload and her synapses weren't firing correctly. She needed to think, and yet this one night she wanted to give up thinking. All she wanted to do was feel, and she was doing a pretty good job of noticing that one of Mitch's hands had cupped the cheek of her ass, the other gripped her hip and was now traveling over her waist, her ribs, and when he covered her breast she gasped into his mouth. His groan against her lips made her tremble.

She rocked against him, her pussy wet and quivering with awakening. It had been so long. She needed a man—just for tonight. Then she could take off the Cinderella ball gown, toss on her shorts and T-shirt and go back to cleaning the castle once again. But tonight, she really wanted to be the princess and enjoy the prince, knowing that she and Mitch were worlds apart, that in a week or so he'd fly off in a corporate jet somewhere, and she'd have wonderful memories of a night spent in his arms, without commitment, without strings. She demanded nothing, and neither would he.

"Please," she whispered, breaking the contact with his delicious mouth.

He pulled his head back. "You sure?"

"Yes." She loved that he asked. Cody had never asked. He'd demanded, he'd taken.

No, she'd promised herself she wouldn't think about him anymore. Ever again. And especially not tonight.

"Come on." He took her hand and led her back toward the bungalow.

She was a little nervous about being so exposed. But he surprised her by bypassing the cabana and taking the little stone steps to the walkway leading back to the hotel.

"My shoes."

"I'll have someone grab them and deliver them to the suite in the morning."

Her stomach fluttered. In the morning. They were spending the night? "Uh, Mitch…"

"I already told your mother I was kidnapping you, and that we might decide to stay over and enjoy an overnight tour of the area. She'll take care of picking up your kids in the morning from Don's and taking care of the motel."

She should be angry that he'd assumed. But she wasn't. He didn't intimate that she was a sure thing, only that she might want to enjoy the sights. He led her into the lobby, then stopped at the desk for a key, thanked the person on duty and they moved toward the elevator. He slid the key card in a slot in the elevator and they rode to the top floor.

"Penthouse?"

He smiled. "I have a suite on the top floor."

She shook her head. Of course he did.

The elevator opened directly onto the suite, which was incredible, luxurious, in blacks and creams with floor to ceiling views of the city and the ocean that she barely had time to gape at because they hadn't moved more than halfway into the main living room before Mitch swept her into his arms again and planted his mouth on hers.

She lost her breath on the first kiss, her body firing up on all cylinders as his hands roamed over the straps of her dress, rolling them over her shoulders then down her arms. Trapped, her arms pinned to her sides, time stopped. She suddenly found herself unable to breathe, her mind lost between the present and the past, remembering all too well that feeling of

Unraveled

being unable to move, of being held, of having choice taken away from her.

No. Don't think about that. This isn't at all like it was with Cody.

But her damn mind wouldn't cooperate. She was breathing too fast, getting lightheaded, her fingertips going numb.

Shit. Not now.

"Greta? Is something wrong?"

Mitch stepped away and she hastily jerked the straps of her dress up right before her knees buckled, the room spinning out of control. He was there to catch her before she crumpled to the floor.

Idiot. Moron. Dumbass. How could she have an attack now, and at this moment?

"Whoa. What's wrong?"

She fought for breath, tried to form words but all she could do was concentrate on sucking in oxygen. Too much oxygen. Slow down. Her face was numb. She wanted to die of embarrassment, to crawl into a hole and disappear.

Mitch's voice was soft and tender as he spoke to her. "Come on. Let's sit you down." He picked her up and carried her to the sofa, set her down and then sat next to her. "Put your head down below your knees."

She knew the drill. Apparently, he did, too.

"Breathe slow, in and out. Concentrate. That's it."

His coaching helped. She followed his instructions, focusing only on the sound of his voice instead of her erratic breathing and shaky body. Soon, she could feel her fingers and toes again. It was working.

"You're not going to fall over, are you? I'm going to get you a glass of water."

She waved her hand and nodded. He left and was back not

more than a minute later.

"Drink this."

Now that her head wasn't spinning, she lifted it slowly, took the glass of water and sipped, letting Mitch hold the glass since her hands were still shaking. "Thank you."

"You're welcome. I brought this, too."

He swept her hair away from her neck and pressed a cold washcloth to her nape. God, that felt so good, swept away the cloying heat her cold sweat had brought on. She spent a few minutes with her hands pressed together in her lap, letting the washcloth ease the overwhelming warmth from her body. When she had it all under control again, she turned her gaze to him. "I'm really sorry, Mitch."

"Don't be. I've seen panic attacks before. Can you lean back now?"

"Yes."

He stood and opened the sliding door to let the cool breeze sweep in. Greta sucked in giant gulps of ocean filled air. With each breath, she felt more normal again. As normal as a moron could feel anyway.

So much for her planned evening of sweet seduction and sex. "Mitch, I can explain."

"I don't think you have to explain anything," he said, his arms folded in front of him as he looked down at her. "He held you down and forced you, didn't he?"

Okay, so she didn't have to explain. She swallowed, not wanting to admit it but figuring she owed him an explanation. "Yes."

He sat next to her on the sofa. "And I got too close, held you too tight, went too fast, and it was just like him. I'm sorry, Greta."

She turned to face him, pulling her legs up on the sofa.

"You did *nothing* wrong. When you pulled my straps down it just triggered a memory of being pinned."

"Shit." Mitch dragged his fingers through his hair. "He tied you up?"

"Sometimes. Only if I wasn't cooperative. Which was a lot toward the end because I wanted nothing to do with him."

Mitch blew out a very loud sigh. "Why didn't you press charges?"

She let her lips curve. "It's never as easy as it seems. Pressing rape charges against your own husband is very difficult to prove. And he wasn't always like that. Just the last year or so, when the drugs took over..."

"It doesn't matter. He had no right."

"No, he didn't. But by then I just wanted out. I wanted him gone. Fortunately, he knew what was coming and he took off before I got the police involved. I got my divorce and got him away from me and the kids."

"Does Don know about this?"

"Oh, God no. Don would have killed him and I couldn't bear that. No matter what he did, he's still the father of my children. I wanted him gone, not dead. Only my mother knew what Cody had done. And once it was over and he had disappeared, I was okay. That's all I really wanted, was to get him away from us."

"Are you sure?"

"I got a restraining order. He can't come near me without being arrested. I haven't seen him for five years. He's supposed to pay child support. Believe me, he doesn't want to be found. He's out of our lives."

He brushed his fingers across her cheek, the gesture so gentle it made her want to cry. "But what about you?"

"I'm fine."

"Are you?"

"Mom paid for quite a few sessions with a rape counselor when she found out what Cody did to me. They helped. They helped a lot."

"That's good."

"And I don't have these panic attacks all that often. It's just that I haven't...been with anyone. I didn't know how I was going to react."

Mitch arched a brow. "You haven't been with anyone...in how long?"

She tipped her gaze to her lap, then back at him. "Since him."

He sighed again, then rubbed his fingers across his brow. "Fuck. I didn't know."

She laughed. "Of course you didn't know."

He shifted, then pulled out his phone. "I'll order the helicopter and we'll take you back home."

Her stomach fell to her feet. "What? Why?"

"Because I don't want to hurt you."

She took the phone out of his hands and set it down on the coffee table in front of them. "I don't want to go home, Mitch. I want to stay here and finish what we started."

He eyed her warily. "Greta. You don't have to do anything you're not ready for. You have nothing to prove."

"I'm not trying to prove anything. And I refuse to let him ruin me. What's done is in the past. It's been five years, Mitch. It's time I move on with my life. And I can't think of a better person to do that with. I trust you. You'll never hurt me like Cody did."

He lifted one strand of her hair and sifted his fingers through it. "No, Greta. I would never hurt you like that."

"Then don't end this night. Please."

He leaned in, pressed his lips to hers, a light, gentle kiss before pulling away.

"Are you sure this is what you want?"

Now it was her turn to lean in. "Yes." She kissed him, rimmed his bottom lip with her tongue, felt the warmth of his breath on her face. "You have no idea how much."

"You have to tell me every step of the way if it's too much for you."

She shuddered out a breath, knowing she'd made the right decision. "I will. Just make love to me, don't treat me like I'm fragile. I won't break, I promise."

Chapter Seven

Mitch stared at Greta, amazed. A woman who'd been through so much, had survived trauma and come through it so strong.

A few minutes ago she'd been in the throes of a hard, gut-wrenching panic attack.

Now, she was asking him to do the one thing to her that caused terror deep in her soul.

Part of him wanted to walk away, didn't want to be the one to hurt her like her ex-husband had. Another part of him craved to be the one to touch her, to show her that not all men were abusive assholes. Because he knew he could do it right. Someone else might not.

And she damn well deserved to have it done right.

God knows he wanted her, had since the first time he laid eyes on her at the motel. And it had nothing to do with wanting to romance the motel out from under her, and everything to do with the softness of her skin, the sweetness of her smile, the way she laughed, the way she made him feel.

He hadn't been this relaxed, hadn't enjoyed a woman's company this much in a long time. Greta was real. He knew more about her in two days than most women he spent months with. Why was that? Because they had a history together?

They really didn't have a history, though. His history was

with her brother. That's who he'd been friends with all those years ago. Yet he knew a lot about Greta. And he wanted to know more.

He stood and held out his hand for her, helping her stand. "Steady on your feet now?"

She nodded. "I'm perfectly fine."

Yeah, she was, beautiful in her silver sparkly dress that showed off her curves and her shapely legs. And she'd worn her hair down tonight, all burnished auburn waves that had caught the light of the setting sun. He reached behind her and undid the clip at the top of her head, then tangled his fingers in those soft curls to bring her face close to his.

He paused, waiting. "You're sure."

"Yes."

"I'm going to undress you, touch you, taste you, fuck you. We're going to do this all night long. I'm going to make you come over and over again, Greta. But I will not hurt you. I know exactly what the word *no* means. Use it if you need to."

She shuddered a breath, her eyes glassy with passion. She nodded, then licked her lips.

He leaned in and brushed his lips across hers. She had an amazing mouth, warm and inviting, her taste sweet. He wanted more, wanted it now, but he tempered his need, remembering that this was her first time after being treated badly by someone who should have cared for her. He was going to take things slow, starting with the kiss. He explored her lips, her tongue, letting her set the pace, letting her tongue dance with his, letting Greta see that she was going to be the one in control tonight. Because that's what she needed. And when she leaned against him, laid her hands on his shoulders, he stepped back, holding on to her hands to guide them both to the sofa. He sat, and let her fall softly on top of him, their lips still connected in a wild dance that made him hard and needy.

She broke the kiss, her lips wet and puffy, her hair in wild disarray. His cock twitched at the way she looked at him, her eyes targeted on his. She pulled off his tie and discarded it on the back of the sofa, then went for the buttons of his shirt, taking her time with each button until he was forced to clench his jaw. She had straddled his lap, her hot pussy in contact with his erection.

She knew it, too, and rocked against him as she undid the buttons, taking glances at his face every time she undid a button.

"You trying to torture me?" he asked.

"I'm torturing us both." Finished with the buttons, she pushed the shirt off his shoulders, pulling at the sleeves until the shirt was gone. Then she went for his belt. At least she was starting to pick up the pace. He was afraid he'd grind his teeth down to the pulp if she didn't hurry up. Once his belt was undone, she released the button on his pants, then reached for the zipper, sliding down his legs so she could pull the zipper down. Her knuckles stroked his shaft as she drew the zipper open, and he groaned. Greta's gaze snapped to his and her lips lifted in a smile.

He reached for her hips and gently raised her to a standing position so he could drop his pants, then his boxers.

She stared at him, from his legs to his cock to his abs to his chest and finally back up at his face.

"You're magnificent," she said in a whisper.

"And you're still dressed."

She grinned. "I can fix that." She turned around. "With your help."

"Gladly." He drew her hair to the side, unable to resist planting a kiss at the nape of her neck. He inhaled the scent of her shampoo, something sweet and floral.

She shivered.

He drew the zipper of her dress down, and she pulled it off and let it drop to her feet, leaving her wearing only tiny black panties.

She turned slowly, and he sucked in a breath at how beautiful she was.

Not model thin or gym sculpted like so many of the women he dated. This woman was real, with full breasts, full hips, and fit from working for a living.

She cocked her head to the side. "I've had two children, Mitch. Be kind."

"I think you're gorgeous." He slid his arms around her waist and pulled her against him for a kiss, letting her know with his mouth and his tongue how very attractive he thought she was. She sighed against him, then whimpered when his erection slid between her legs to tease her panty-clad pussy.

The scent of her arousal filled the air around them, a heady scent that drove him to near insanity. He had to taste her, to touch her, to get her spread-eagled on his bed and show her that she could be pleasured without being hurt. He scooped her up in his arms and carried her through the living room and down the hall into his bedroom, leaving the light off. The drapes were open, the moon casting plenty of light on the room. He deposited her on the bed and went to the doors, opening them to let a breeze in, then came back to her.

"Scoot to this edge of the bed, babe."

She did, without hesitation, showing her trust. He liked that. He reached for her panties and she lifted her hips, allowing him to slide them down her legs and off.

Bare, she was beautiful, a tuft of curls covering the top of her sex. Otherwise, her clit and pussy lips were full and plump and glistening with the sweet cream he intended to lick from her. His balls tightened at the thought of everything he wanted to do with her tonight. It was the patience that was going to be difficult, especially when she leaned back on her elbows and stared up at him with a half smile, expectation and fear spread across her features.

He went to her, laying his palms flat on the bed on either side of her. Without touching her body with his hands, he pressed his lips to one shoulder. She turned her head and watched as he moved his mouth across her collarbone, then down to capture one pink nipple.

She sucked in a loud breath as he caught her nipple between his teeth and wrapped his tongue around it, then pulled it fully into his mouth. He used his hand then, cupping the breast, holding it while he feasted on her flesh until she arched her back and fed him more. He used his other hand to pluck the nipple of her other breast until he moved his mouth to that one.

Greta dropped her head to the mattress, closed her eyes, and allowed him to love her breasts, her nipples, until they were sharp, tight points. Then he kissed her ribcage, her belly, and she opened her eyes again, watching his progress down to her lower belly. He teased her belly button and she laughed, reaching out to tangle her fingers in his hair.

He smelled her. Sweet, potent, like honey that he couldn't resist. He dropped to his knees and spread her legs apart, pulled her to the edge of the bed, and took a long swipe with his tongue.

Greta let out a low moan, and shuddered, then lifted her butt, silently asking for more. He smiled, and leaned forward, covering her sex with his mouth. He took her clit between his lips and flicked it with his tongue, swirled around the tight bud, then lapped it, all the while watching her reaction, feeling the hot moisture surround his face.

"Mitch. Oh, God, Mitch, that feels so good." She tightened her hold on his hair as he licked the length of her, sliding his tongue inside her to taste her fully, then brought his fingers in to play with her clit while he licked her pussy.

She came in a burst of moans and lifts and hot cream. He held her while she bucked against him and gave him more than he could ever ask for. When she settled, he kissed her inner thighs, licked her clean, then climbed up her body, rolling onto his back on the bed so he could pull her on top of him. This first time, he wanted her to have all the control.

Panting, she bent down and kissed him, licked his lips. She smiled down at him and he loved the contented look on her face.

"Wow."

He pulled her hair away from her face and drew her mouth to his for another kiss. "I need to be inside you. Condoms are on the nightstand."

She reached over, pulled out a packet and handed it to him. He put on the condom and she straddled him, placing her hands on his chest while she settled on his cock.

Seething heat surrounded him as she slid over him, finally seated fully on him. He reached up to slide his palms over the hard peaks of her breasts as Greta began to rock back and forth against him, setting her own rhythm, dragging her clit against his pelvis.

He lifted, driving his cock deeper inside her, holding on to her hips but letting her take charge, not wanting to direct her or in any way make her feel like he was holding her down.

She didn't seem at all tense or nervous, instead focused on the two of them joined together, exactly the way he wanted her to be. She tilted her head back and rode him hard, her pussy squeezing his cock in a tight vise. He bit his lip as he watched this beautiful woman undulate against him. His balls tightened, filled, ready to burst, but he needed to hold back, wanting her to go again.

She dug her nails into his chest, dipped forward, her gaze

shooting into his. He felt the spasms inside her and knew she was going to come again.

"That's it, come on," he urged, rocking upward, giving her more as she slid back and forth.

She held on to his gaze as she let go, her pussy contracting around him in waves. And he let go too, digging his fingers into her hips and watching her beautiful face as he came in hot, hard torrents.

Greta collapsed onto his chest and he wrapped his arms around her, still shuddering with the aftereffects of what had been one incredible orgasm. He stroked her back, listened to her breathe, and kissed her sweat-dampened face. She finally rolled off and he stepped into the bathroom to clean up, then came back and rolled back onto the bed, pulling her into his arms. She laid her head on his shoulder, her palm against his chest.

He felt...content. Weirdly content. Like, not at all in a hurry to get this woman out of his suite, which was usually the case. He wanted to hold her in his arms all night.

"Thank you, Mitch. That was something I had to face, but I've been afraid to for so long. You made it...incredible."

"It was pretty incredible for me, too." He kissed the top of her head.

"I'm sure you have lots of sex. You don't have to say that."

"I'm not Hugh Hefner, Greta. I don't have a harem of women flocking to see to my every need."

She lifted her head. "You don't? My illusions are shattered."

He laughed and she laid her head down again.

"So now what?" she asked.

"Now we rest for a few minutes, and then we do it again."

"Oh good. I haven't done all night sex in...okay never."

He liked knowing that. He rolled to his side and pulled her

to face him. "I'll call room service and order coffee. You're going to be up all night."

Chapter Eight

It was warm this afternoon. Greta was sweaty and the sun beat incessantly down on her body. Being so close to the roof of the motel wasn't helping cool her down any, either. But the job needed to be done, she'd put it off long enough. Decorations had to go up, and that included lights around the motel.

"Festive."

She shot her gaze down at Mitch who looked cool and unruffled in his board shorts and white tank top.

"Ho, ho, ho." She hung another light to the hook.

"Want me to help you?"

"No, thanks. I've got it covered."

"Wouldn't it go faster with some help?"

She blew out a breath and stared down at him. "Shouldn't you be at the Hyatt or Westin or something?"

He grinned. "I like this place."

"No you don't. You just like irritating me."

"Sheesh. Use a guy for sex one night, discard him the next day." He shook his head.

After a horrified glance around to make sure no one was around to hear him, she laughed, then flushed all over, remembering the night before. She'd tucked away her beautiful silver dress, convinced she was never going to wear it again, then put on her drudge clothes. The ball was over for this Cinderella. "I'm hardly the type to use and discard. Especially after only one use."

"So, you're saying you're a recycler."

"Uh huh."

"I'll hold you to that."

Her body flamed, but it wasn't from the hot sun. "You do that. Now go away and let me work."

He disappeared, and she went back to hanging lights, but almost fell off the ladder about ten minutes later when she saw him appear on the roof, walking up from the other side.

"What are you doing up there?"

He leaned over and helped her drag up the lights, deftly grabbing and latching them onto the hooks. "I told you, I'm helping."

"You can't. What if you fall off?"

He cocked his head to the side. "I never fall off."

"My liability insurance won't cover it, Mitch. I'm serious."

"I have plenty of insurance. Quit worrying."

Exasperated, she let him complete the other side while she finished the one she'd started.

"This is a little different than what you normally do, isn't it?" she asked.

He lifted his head. "Huh?"

"Board rooms, million dollar deals, fancy hotels and probably a supermodel on your arm while you're in a tux drinking champagne. Not quite the same thing as hanging off the roof of a beaten down old motel putting up old Christmas lights."

He stared at her until she grew uncomfortable. "Greta. I grew up here, remember? My parents lived in the same two-bedroom house for forty years. The house I painted myself three times. Not a great house, either. I used to climb up on my beat-up roof and hang old Christmas lights every year."

She'd forgotten that young Mitch ever existed. All she saw now was the flash, the money. The millionaire. "I'm sorry."

"Don't be. But don't ever forget that I know what it's like to be without money. And don't look down on me just because I have it now. Because I busted my ass to get where I am."

She nodded, feeling awful. "Okay."

He slid his thumb across her cheek. "No tears or I'll have to drag you off that ladder and kiss you. Then what would the people on the beach think?"

She laughed and they went back to work. The job was completed in half the time thanks to his assistance. When she climbed down the ladder, he was right there to fold it and put it away in storage.

"Why are you doing this, Mitch?"

"Doing what?" he asked, storing the ladder on its side, then closing and locking the storage facility.

"Work. At my motel."

He shrugged. "Nothing better to do. Though your mom is bringing the kids back later for more surfing lessons."

Hands on her hips, she said, "You don't have to do that, either."

"I want to. I like your kids, Greta."

She cocked a brow. "Why do I feel like there's some ulterior motive in everything you do?"

"I don't know. I'm pretty direct about what I want. You know I want to buy your motel and I'll keep trying to convince you, but I'll be very up front about that. I don't believe in underhanded tactics or subterfuge. I keep my business separate from personal."

She felt bad for even thinking it. "Sorry."

"You should be. I'm here because I want to be. This is a stretch of beach I remember fondly from when I was a kid. I like it. I like being around your kids, too." He leaned in a pressed a kiss to her bare shoulder. "And I especially like being around you."

She shuddered, stepping into the house. "You're bad for me."

Mitch shut the door behind him, locked it, and leaned her against the wall. "Yeah? How so?"

Her pussy swelled, moisture coating her panties. Just like that, she was aroused, ready, needy. "Because you make me want things I shouldn't."

He leaned in and pressed his lips against her neck. "Yeah? Like what?"

When he licked the column of her throat, her legs buckled. "Like that."

His hand covered her breast, pulled aside the material of her bikini top to cover her flesh, pluck at her nipple. He followed the action by dipping down and taking the already pulsing bud between his lips, devouring her with his hungry mouth until she banged her head against the wall. He turned his head to look at her, his eyes hard with passion.

"Mitch." His name fell from her lips in a throaty whisper that spoke of how deep in the throes of passion she was. He reached behind her and untied the strings of her bikini top, discarded it, filled his hands with her breasts, focusing on her face as he plucked at her nipples until her body burned. He had her wedged between himself and the wall, his knee between her legs, but she didn't mind this, had the freedom for her hands to roam over the exposed flesh of his shoulder, could push him back if she wanted to.

Oh, she didn't want to, in fact wanted to draw him closer,

to feel the heat of his cock heavy and hard against her. As far as she was concerned, there was way too much distance between them. Those few inches of separation felt like miles.

"More," she whispered, pulling at his shirt to bring his mouth back to hers, his body in direct contact with all her pleasure points. His lips on hers, his body settled against hers, his cock rocking between her legs, only ratcheted up her craving for more.

She tore at his shirt, lifting it up to pull it over his head. He got her message loud and clear, undoing the strings of his board shorts. She watched him undress while she pushed her own shorts and panties down, kicked them to the side, spreading her legs, needing him with a desperation that bordered on insanity.

Maybe she was insane, out of her mind with this wild desire that had taken hold and gripped her from the inside out, making her lose all common sense. What was she doing making love with Mitch in the middle of the day?

Having fun. You're having fun, Greta. Let go.

He applied a condom, then he was there again, his skin touching her skin, his mouth on hers. He reached behind her to cup her bottom and arch her toward him, lifted one of her legs over his hip and used his hand to guide his cock toward her center, then tilted his head back.

"This okay for you?"

"Yes," was all she could manage before palming the back of his head and taking his mouth while at the same time he slid his cock inside her.

Yes! That's what she needed, Mitch buried deep. She pulsed around him, the heat of her body swelling to an inferno, her pussy surrounding him as he pulled back and slid deeper inside her. And then he lifted her off the floor and she wrapped both legs around his back, riding his cock while he held her, pushing her against the wall as he slammed into her again and again. He lifted her higher so he could take her nipples into his mouth, licking them, sucking them, driving her crazy with sensation that shot pleasure through her nerve endings.

"Look at me, Greta."

She met his gaze, and it was raw, filled with passion, the same need she felt swirling like a vortex inside her. It was so emotional, so incredibly erotic to see passion reflected in his eyes, to know that he felt what she felt.

She tightened, feeling the first strains of orgasm build deep within.

"That's it," he said, his jaw clenched tight, his fingers digging into her ass cheeks as he ground against her, splintering her. "I'm going to come, Greta. Come with me."

Her breathing went erratic, but this time it wasn't panic causing the heaping gulps of air she sucked in. It was giant pulses of bliss that zapped her from the inside out, tearing her apart as intense bursts of lightning-like pleasure gripped her in the throes of a climax that made her cry out and dig her nails into Mitch's shoulders.

He groaned, shuddered, pumping harder as her pussy spasmed around his cock in wave after wave, until she finally relaxed, the pulses lessening. Mitch eased his grip on her. He let her legs down and she touched the floor, but realized she had no balance, no strength. Mitch rested his forehead against hers and they both took long, deep breaths.

"It's a good thing I'm in good shape or you might just kill me."

She laughed. They disengaged and went into her bathroom to clean up. She couldn't help staring at Mitch's body as she watched him soap up in the shower. He caught her looking and grinned.

"Sorry. It's been a long dry spell for me," she said. "You

might be in trouble if you hang around me."

He turned her around and soaped her back. "That's the kind of trouble I don't mind."

And she wouldn't mind having him hanging around, which really wasn't a good thing.

Because she knew it was only temporary. Soon enough, he'd be leaving. And the last thing she needed to do was become involved, attached, or in any way emotional about Mitch Magruder.

Mitch was becoming attached. That wasn't good for business.

But after spending the morning with Greta, and then the afternoon surfing again with her kids, he realized that it would be so easy to just...hang out with them. With all of them.

He liked kids just fine, and they always seemed to like him, but he didn't necessarily feel a need to spend a lot of time with them. The thing was, he really liked Jeff and Zoey, had a natural affection for both of them that had seemed to develop instantly. The three of them had bonded, they talked about anything and everything, and damn those kids were smart. And fun. They had no fear of the water, and hell, what wasn't there to like about that?

But he worried about them, about their futures, almost like a...parent.

He wasn't their father. The damn irritating thing was, they had no father. The man who should be responsible for them had bailed. And that wasn't right.

Greta was a wonderful mother, had made a ton of sacrifices for her kids, but he knew they needed more.

He could give them more, but what right did he have to interfere?

If she'd just accept his offer...

"You must be planning a huge deal."

He turned at the sound of Don's voice. He'd asked Don to meet him at Rusty's Bar for a beer this afternoon. They shook hands and Mitch signaled the waitress for two cold ones. "I'm always planning a huge deal."

"That must be what put that look in your eyes. I know it wasn't Greta agreeing to sell the Crystal Sands."

"You know your sister that well, huh?"

Don laughed and accepted the bottle of beer the waitress set in front of him, took a long swallow and leaned back in the wide wood chair. "She thinks of that old rundown bucket of wood and nails as a monument to our old man. I loved our dad too, but she was Daddy's little girl. And when he left her that motel, she took it as a sign that he wanted her to keep it as some kind of memorial to him."

"Did he?"

Don shook his head and took another pull of his beer before answering. "I doubt it. Dad loved the Crystal Sands. He always had big plans for that place. Then again he had big plans for a lot of his projects."

"Like the fishing and boating business."

Don nodded. "Fortunately, that's a pretty lucrative piece of the pie. And I've been able to grow the business by adding a couple more boats and building onto the pier. Greta has no capital."

"I've offered."

"I know, I know," Don said, raising his hand. "But her thought processes are different. She's sentimental. She doesn't like change. And Cody...man, that sonofabitch did a number on her, Mitch."

"She told me some of it."

"He held the wallet. Managed the finances, controlled every penny she spent, where she was allowed to go. He laid a thumb over her."

As strong a personality as Greta was, he couldn't fathom her abiding that. "How did she put up with it?"

"I don't know," Don said, dragging his fingers through his thinning hair. "She put up with a ton of shit from that prick, all to protect the kids. He threatened them, threatened her that he'd take the kids and disappear. The best thing that ever happened to her was the day he left and agreed to the divorce."

"Asshole." Mitch made a mental note to track down Cody Mason and make his life a living hell.

"Anyway, after Dad died and gave her the motel, she finally had something that no one could take from her. So now she holds on to that motel like it's the only thing of value in her life. That and her kids. Because they're hers."

He nodded, understanding how she felt. Still, he could offer her so much more. But maybe this time, it wasn't going to be about what he wanted. Even though he'd never once lost out on a deal, maybe this was one he should walk away from.

Even if it wasn't in Greta's best interests.

He sipped his beer and pondered his options.

"Mitch."

He looked over at Don. "Yeah?"

"I know you want the property and the land. And you and I go way back. But don't hurt my sister. She's been through enough."

"Yeah, she has."

"Look, man, I love you like a brother, you know that. But I love her more. And if it comes down to choosing between the two of you, I think you know where I'll stand."

Mitch nodded, glad that Greta had a man like Don backing

her up. "I would never hurt her, Don." In fact, he was going to do whatever it took to help her. Even if that meant losing what he wanted.

Chapter Nine

Somehow, it worked out that Greta's children had both been asked to spend the night at their friend's houses, and Mitch had invited Greta out to dinner again. This time, he said there was a Christmas party at the mayor's house.

The mayor's house! She'd never been there, even though she was a member of the Chamber of Commerce. But sure, let a millionaire swoop into town for the holidays, and he garners an instant invitation to the mayor's annual Christmas party.

She'd had time to run to the mall and buy a nice black dress, refusing to let Mitch outfit her for this soiree. The dress was expensive and not at all in her budget, but as soon as she'd tried it on she knew she had to have it. Sleek and silky, it fit her perfectly. It had cap sleeves and a silver band embedded across the empire waist. The dress flowed out right at the knee in kicky little waves. She loved it and had to admit it looked gorgeous. Besides, a black dress was something she could wear again and again. Just in case the mayor took a liking to her and decided to invite her to the party next year.

She laughed at that, hung crystal drop earrings on her ears, and slipped on the shoes Mitch had given her which went great with the dress—no sense in buying new shoes when these were so versatile.

Mitch arrived on time wearing a dark suit with a red tie and looking devastatingly handsome as usual. Whether in surf shorts or tux or anything in between, the man took her breath away. He cupped her chin, giving her a soft kiss. She melted.

"You look beautiful," he said. "That dress is stunning."

Her face warmed. She wasn't used to compliments, or attention of any kind. She'd lived wrapped up in a cocoon of work and her kids for years, and felt like a butterfly spreading its wings in the few days she'd been around Mitch. "You're good for my ego," she said. "And you look incredible."

He grinned. "Thanks. Ready to go?"

She was shocked to see a white stretch limousine with blacked out windows parked in front of the motel. Her gaze snapped to Mitch. He grinned.

"Thought you'd want to arrive at the mayor's house in style."

She laughed, climbed in, and marveled that the inside of the limo was big enough to live in. Television, long bench seats, full bar, it was luxurious and utterly decadent.

The mayor lived at the top of the hill in town, in an old white mansion that had been redecorated by one of the top interior designers in the country. Greta had seen pictures of it in the state magazine, but she'd always wanted to get a glimpse of it in person, so she was excited that she was actually going to be able to do so tonight.

It didn't disappoint. Parquet flooring in geometric patterns greeted them in the entry. As they moved inside, Greta stared slack jawed at marble statues, granite countertops in the kitchens and state of the art appliances, objects d'art spread throughout the pristine marble floors of the dining hall, thick white columns and plush carpeting you could sleep on. She continued to gape as Mayor Thomas Jefferson Patterson gave them a tour of his marvelous home. She hoped she wasn't drooling.

"Of course, I know your hotels are five star all the way,"

Mayor Patterson said to Mitch as they walked out to the gardens. "So I hope you can appreciate the work we put into the mansion."

"You've done an amazing job," Mitch said, keeping his hand tightly held to Greta's.

"It's lovely, Mayor Patterson."

He smiled at Greta. "Thank you, Mrs. Mason. And how is your little motel on the beach doing?"

Little motel on the beach. How...patronizing. "It's doing just fine, thank you. We'll be nearly full by Christmas."

"Lovely. Word around town is that there was a recent offer to build a resort on your land, and that you refused to sell."

Uh-oh. Her gaze shot to Mitch, and he shook his head. She didn't think the information had come from him. He might want her hotel, but he wouldn't exactly send out a press release about it.

"I'm happy with the motel the way it is, Mayor."

Mayor Patterson turned to her and sniffed. He might be influential and popular, but he was also a pompous ass. "Mrs. Mason, do you have any idea what a resort of that caliber could do for the residents of Ft. Lincoln Beach? The other business owners in this town? The revenue, the tax dollars? The improvements we could make in our city would be beyond belief. You're holding back progress, my dear, and I don't understand why."

"But it's my choice to make, and it's my property, Mayor." She smiled tightly and Mitch squeezed her hand.

"Your motel is ancient. It needs work. You're never at full capacity and barely meet code."

She inhaled, knowing she'd never be able to explain to him that she loved the Crystal Sands just the way it was, the way her father had left it to her. "I'm not interested in having my motel demolished, Mayor. Perhaps whoever is interested in buying up ocean front property can look elsewhere."

The mayor narrowed his gaze and lowered his voice. "You know very well that's a prime location. You're simply being stubborn for no reason."

"I think Greta is perfectly able to make her own decision about her future and that of her business, Mayor," Mitch said, the clipped tone of his voice indicating that the mayor had stepped out of line.

Mayor Patterson took a quick step back and plastered a smile back on his face.

"Of course, of course. And it's Christmas, so we won't discuss business tonight. Come, let's have some punch."

Asshole. He'd already discussed business and made his opinion clear. He thought she was getting in the way of town progress. Great. Just what she needed—more guilt.

"Ignore him," Mitch said as the mayor went off to greet more guests. "We're just here for free food and drinks."

She laughed. "He's been ignoring me for years. I guess I can try to return the favor."

Mitch slid her hand in the crook of his arm and led her into the house. "That's my girl."

Some of her excitement over being at the mayor's house diminished after talking to him, but she refused to let him completely dampen her enthusiasm. After all, she rarely got a night out, and never dressed up like this. Since Mitch had arrived in Ft. Lincoln Beach, she'd done so twice in one week. She intended to enjoy every minute of it. This was her chance to mix and mingle with other business owners in town, the opportunity to trade ideas about growing their respective businesses—especially her own. She wanted more people to stay at her motel, and if she could get some of the other businesses in town to send people her way, to carry her advertising, then it would be worth having to listen to the snooty mayor look down his nose at her and criticize the decisions she made.

Unfortunately, as she attempted to mingle with the other guests over drinks and dinner, she ran into the same unwelcome topic.

"You won't sell the motel, Greta? Why not? It's old, run down, needs major refurbishing."

"No amount of paint and rehab will help the old Crystal Sands, Greta. You need to sell and sell now. You must have been offered a fortune for that old place. Are you insane for turning down that kind of money?"

"Greta. Sell. What are you thinking? You're holding us all back."

Everyone knew about the offer to buy the motel, and everyone was stunned she had turned it down. They all saw it as a prime growth opportunity for the town, and saw Greta as the evil monster who was holding back progress—and revenue—for everyone.

Shit.

None of them understood why, and she wasn't about to try and explain it to them. They wouldn't care. The few friends she'd made in the business community were now turning their backs on her. Money was more powerful than friendship, apparently. And she was taking revenue out of their pockets by refusing growth.

Her evening sailed south in a hurry, though she tried to put on a brave front for Mitch. He had just been doing what he did best—buy up non-revenue producing properties to build his gorgeous resorts. He brought thriving commerce into communities. That was his business.

He was a savior. Everyone loved him.

Conversely, everyone hated her, especially here at the

mayor's mansion tonight.

"Can we go?" she finally asked after dinner when she couldn't tolerate the silent, devil-eyed glares of her peers any longer. "I have a terrible headache."

Mitch frowned in concern and smoothed his hand down her back. "Of course. I'll go get your coat."

She shrank against the front door, trying to look invisible while Mitch stopped to talk to the mayor and a couple others who whispered in his ear, shooting pointed looks in her direction the entire time. By the time he returned with her jacket, his expression was grim. He helped her with her coat, left his hand pressed to the small of her back, and escorted her out the door to the waiting limo.

The ride was silent, Greta lost in her thoughts.

She was making the right decision in sticking to her guns. She knew she was. Dad would never want the Crystal Sands to be anything more than what it had always been. A nice family-run place. Small, comfortable, not a resort monster like the kind of places Mitch built.

"You don't owe them any explanation, Greta," Mitch said after they'd left. "Nor an apology for the decisions you make."

She stared down at her lap. "They hate me."

He laughed, and she whipped her head up to look at him.

"Honey, there isn't a day goes by that a decision I make doesn't make someone wish for my immediate demise. In business, sometimes you make unpopular decisions."

"But you don't make the kinds of choices that have everyone in your town despise you."

"They'll get over it."

"I doubt it. I probably won't be welcome at the grocery store or local mall anymore."

"I think you're overexaggerating."

"This is a small town, Mitch. Everyone knows everyone else. Word will get out that I single handedly halted major progress."

"One hotel would not be responsible for a growth explosion in Ft. Lincoln Beach. Every retailer in town would have to pony up improvements and expansions to their own facilities."

"They don't see it that way. Steps two and three can't happen without step one, and that's where I squashed the entire thing." Guilt stomped around in her stomach, mashing the delicious lobster she'd had for dinner.

"You have to stop carrying the world on your shoulders. If it's anyone's fault, it's mine."

She frowned. "Yours? Why?"

"I should have been more low key, should have approached you directly. I'd forgotten about small-town gossip."

She waved her hand. "That's not for you to worry about. I can handle it."

"You handle everything by yourself, don't you?"

He'd said it like an accusation, though his voice was soft.

"I have to, Mitch. I'm responsible for my children."

"You're a remarkable woman, Greta. You have more strength than you give yourself credit for. I admire you."

She snorted. "Yeah, I'm just superwoman, aren't I?"

"In many ways, you're one of the strongest women I've ever met."

She didn't know what to say in answer to that, just stared into his cool blue eyes and got lost in the warmth of his smile. She snuggled against him and decided to enjoy the end of the night with Mitch, since the beginning and middle had been utterly forgettable.

It took her awhile to realize Mitch wasn't taking her back to her motel. They were coasting up the highway next to the beach.

"Where are we going?" she asked.

"Nowhere." He reached into the bar to pull out a bottle of champagne. He uncorked it and popped it open, then filled two glasses with the bubbling liquid and handed one to her. "I thought we'd take a ride."

She watched the white surf go by as they rode leisurely from town to town and sipped champagne, feeling decadent and so like a fish out of water. Did he have any idea how out of her element this all was? "This is not my lifestyle, Mitch."

He took a long swallow, emptied the glass and set it down, then turned to her. "It could be."

Her smile died as frustration filled her. She thought they'd never have to have this conversation again. "I'm not selling."

He took the glass away from her. "That's not at all what I'm talking about."

She frowned. "I don't understand."

"Don't you?" He swept his knuckles against her cheek, then slid his arm around her waist to draw her closer, bringing his head down to hers. He brushed her lips with a faint kiss, and she tasted tart champagne, smelled his crisp, clean soap, inhaled the fragrance of the man she'd grown all too close to way too fast. In seconds, the disastrous night melted away, replaced instead by a rush of need for this man, this moment.

He could make her forget, but more importantly, she simply loved being held and touched by him. There was only one problem.

"Mitch."

He leaned in, nuzzled her neck, causing pinpricks of delicious sensation to pop out over her skin. "Yeah."

She reached out to grab his shoulders, conscious of the driver up front. "We're not alone."

Without pulling away from her neck, he reached behind her

and pressed a button. A black screen coasted slowly upward, cutting them off from the driver. "Now we are. He can't see or hear us, and he's been ordered to drive until I tell him to take us back."

She shuddered when his lips found hers again, leaned back in the roomy seat. Mitch followed, his body covering hers. He lifted his head. "Is this too confining for you?"

She hadn't even thought about it. With Mitch, she never felt restrained—in any way. "No. I need to feel you pressed against me."

He slid one hand underneath to cup her bottom, raising it up, aligning her sex against his cock and making her ache even more. He drove against her, making her feel like a teenager in the throes of first passion.

Maybe she was, because she didn't remember ever being fired up like this, ever becoming so aroused so quickly. He rained kisses over her face, down her neck, sucking gently against her throat until her skin was covered in goose bumps. She reached for his shoulder, but contact with his clothes wasn't what she wanted under her hands. She whimpered in frustration and Mitch lifted, hauling her to a sitting position.

"Ever been naked in a limo, Greta?"

His wicked smile and the devilish twinkle in his eyes emboldened her. She pulled off her shoes and dropped to her knees on the carpeted floor, then spread his legs to climb between them. "I haven't been in a limo before."

He shrugged off his jacket.

"Are you going to get naked in here?" she asked, reaching up to take off his tie and toss it on the long bench to her side, then rested her hands on his thighs.

"Would you like me to?"

"Yes."

He unbuttoned his shirt, then pulled it off. When he started on his pants, she brushed his hands aside. "Let me."

His gaze swept to hers, then he leaned back in the seat and she undid his belt, the button, and went for his zipper. His cock was hard, straining against her fingers as she drew the zipper down. She was conscious of Mitch watching her every move, but she was concentrating on drawing his pants apart, pulling them over his hips and down his legs, baring his body to her view, her touch, her mouth.

She'd been dreaming about having access to him. He'd done some amazing things to her body. Now it was her turn to explore, though she wondered about doing this now. Maybe it wasn't the right time.

She gazed over her shoulder, but Mitch leaned forward and turned her chin to face him. "We have all the time in the world. It's just you and me."

He resumed his position, leaning back against the buttery soft leather and opening his body to her.

"Take your dress off," he said, the command spoken in a darkly soft voice that thrilled her, so unlike when Cody used to order her around. Probably because she knew she could tell Mitch no and there would be no repercussions. He would never hurt her, never berate her or smack her around just because she had a mind and opinion of her own. And in his command was a request, a need—his need. She lifted the clingy dress over her head and tossed it to the side, leaving her in the plunging satin and lace bra and matching panties.

Mitch's eyes went smoky. "Nice." He palmed his cock and began to stroke it, an act so incredibly erotic all she could do was watch. "Now take off your bra."

He made her want to strip for him, a bold act utterly new to her. She stretched up and reached behind her, making sure to take her time releasing the hooks, then pulling the straps down.

She held the cups against her breasts, watching Mitch's jaw clench, the way he gripped his cock at the base of the shaft and held his fingers there as she pulled the bra away from her breasts. Just as he touched himself, she did the same, cupping her breasts, using her thumbs and fingers to swirl over her nipples. Touching herself had never been as exciting as it was this night. She'd never done it in front of a man before, but doing it for Mitch aroused her, because she could see it turned him on.

"I like that."

She smiled, pushed back and sat on the edge of the long bench across from him, spreading her legs slightly apart. With one hand still on her breast, she slid the other hand down the front of her panties. She heard his indrawn breath as she cupped her sex, using her fingers to slide over her clit, surprising even herself with the heat and pleasure that swelled there. Her lips parted and she whimpered a breathy moan.

Mitch resumed stroking his cock while Greta half reclined on her seat, her hand buried in her panties. She slid two fingers inside her pussy, using the heel of her hand to grind against her clit. With every movement she became further entrenched in the fantasy, in her aroused state, her body in tune with what she was doing, her mind awash in the awareness of Mitch's actions.

Until he half stood and moved toward her. She reached for him, pulling his hips toward her face. He leaned against the side of the seat, his cock near her lips. She scooted over to the edge and inhaled the musky scent of his sex, licking her lips and tilting her head to watch his face.

"Suck me," he whispered, palming her belly, pushing her fingers out of the way to slide his hand inside her panties, replacing her frantic movements with deft, slow caresses of his own. When he cupped her sex, she gasped, and his cock slid between her parted lips. She accepted him greedily, her tongue wrapping around the soft mushroomed head, allowing Mitch to push inside her mouth and feed her his shaft while at the same time he tucked two fingers inside her pussy and began to pump, circling his thumb over her swollen, aching clit.

The pleasure was sweet, unbearable, a vortex of sensation. Tasting him, feeling his fingers inside her, watching the way his eyes, half-lidded in his own pleasure, focused on her as she bobbed over his swollen, hot cock, was overwhelming to her senses, to her body. She felt her orgasm build, more than she could hold back.

Mitch must have felt it too, because he began to pump harder, using the flat of his hand to glide along her wet sex, giving her just the right movement to sail her right over the edge. She arched against his hand and he withdrew his cock, taking her mouth in a deep kiss as she climaxed in hard spasms against his fingers. He held her, kissing her deeply, until the tremors subsided, then moved over her, pulled her panties off, applied a condom and dragged her to the edge of the seat.

He slid inside her with one easy thrust, holding on to her hips, his gaze glued to her face. She was still pulsing inside, her body gripping him in a tight fist of contractions, as if it knew him well, welcomed him and didn't want to let go.

She knew exactly how it felt. She held on to his forearms as he began to thrust harder, wrapped her legs around his back, meeting his force with her own, wanting him deeper, for some reason needing to feel him as far inside her as he could go.

"Damn," he said, sweat pouring off him as their slickened bodies slid together.

Greta shifted, pushing Mitch away, but only so she could change positions. She turned to face the bench seat, giving Mitch her backside. He smoothed his hands reverently over her ass, then used his knees to widen her legs and entered her from behind, pressing her thighs against the seat as the tempo increased.

"Yes!" she cried. This was deeper, this was harder, this was what she needed. She felt every inch of him inside her, his balls bumping her clit as he rammed her with what seemed like the same desperate need she felt—the need for more.

And when he reached around and cupped his hand over her sex, massaging her clit, she felt the squeezing pleasure of coming on his cock, wishing there could be no barrier between them, that her juices could flow on him without the condom, that his come could fill her, could shoot inside her as he rocked and groaned and came in gulping waves.

He fell against her back, kissing her damp nape, whispering romantic words to her. They finally pulled apart, cleaning up to the best of their abilities. Mitch pulled her to one of the long couches and they stretched out to have a cold glass of mineral water.

"Are you just going to let that poor man drive up and down the coast all night long?" she asked.

Mitch traced the valley between her breasts with his fingertip. "He's paid extremely well for the time he works. Believe me, he's not complaining."

She shook her head, but smiled, feeling utterly decadent. What an amazing lifestyle this man led. So unlike hers. She wondered if he—

Well, she wasn't going to wonder what he'd done in a limo and with whom. That wasn't her business. She only knew she'd had a great time with him tonight. And that she was content.

She'd have to be content. This was fun, and she had to keep it just fun. Not monumental, not life changing. Not forever. Just fun.

Just for now.

Chapter Ten

Mitch had directed the limo to one of his hotels in Daytona Beach, gotten them a room, and they'd climbed into bed, shared an amazing room-service meal, made love again, and promptly passed out. He'd made sure they got up early the next morning to make the drive back to the motel. She'd truly felt like Cinderella.

Unfortunately, every time Greta tried to play Cinderella, the damn castle reared its ugly head and slapped her into reality.

Said reality intruded the next day when Greta arrived back at the motel to face an overflowing toilet in Room Four.

Fortunately, her mother had been there to deal with the immediate crisis.

"I shut the water off in there," her mother said. "I didn't call a plumber, figuring you'd want to tackle it yourself first like you always do."

"You figured right." Plumbers cost an arm and a leg, and she always liked to try and fix things herself first before incurring the cost.

So much for being a fairy princess. It was time for Cinderella to change back into her scullery clothes and dive elbows deep in plumbing and water.

She turned to Mitch, who despite being up nearly all night with her still looked gorgeous in his slightly wrinkled suit and shirt and a day's growth of beard stubble across his strong jaw.

"I'm sorry. I need to see to this."

"No problem." He cupped her chin and leaned in to kiss her. "I'll see you in a bit."

He walked away before she could utter a word, but the cough behind her told her that her mother had seen that. "I'm going to change clothes," she said without looking at her mother.

"Obviously you had a really nice time last night," her mother said as Greta hurried down the hall to her front door.

She'd had an amazing time last night, none of which she was going to tell her mother about. But that was last night, and today she was back to being Greta Mason, motel owner. She'd had a fantasy last night. Today was reality, and reality meant bills to pay, a motel to run, and problems to deal with.

She went into the house, dashed into the bedroom and took off her dress and jewelry, once again putting Cinderella's silver shoes into the back of the closet. She smiled at the realization that she'd gotten to wear them twice in one week. Maybe she'd wear them again for Christmas. Then, probably never again.

She grabbed a pair of old shorts and a stained T-shirt, knowing the toilet problem was going to be messy work, put her hair into a ponytail, then slid on her flip flops and headed back into the office to pull a bucket, mop and her tools from the supply room before heading out front toward the room with the plumbing problem.

"Uh, Greta—"

"Not now, Mom. Let me handle Room Four first. Then we'll deal with whatever other catastrophe has popped up." She hoped it wasn't a huge one.

"You don't understand..."

"Seriously, Mom. I can only tackle one problem at a time."

She slipped out the door, master key in her pocket, and pushed through the double entry doors, wishing her idyllic fantasy night could have lingered. No such luck, though.

Head down, she'd made it past Room Two before she saw the plumbing truck and the door to Room Four open.

What the hell?

"I was trying to tell you," her mother said from over her shoulder.

Greta whipped around. "Mom, you know the deal. I try to fix things first around here. Then if all else fails, we call in help."

Her mother smiled. "I didn't call in a plumber, Greta."

"Then who did?"

Her mother arched a brow, grinned, and directed her gaze over Greta's left shoulder. She turned, and there was Mitch. It didn't take much of a stretch to make the connection between him and Ace Plumbing Company's truck.

"You must have some serious connections. I was only inside my house for fifteen minutes."

He shrugged. "I figured you had enough to deal with. I didn't want to see you with your head in the toilet this morning."

Despite his charming grin, she was irritated. "I can handle the crises of my motel by myself, without your interference."

"I'm paying for it."

"I don't need or want your money."

"Greta. That's not gracious."

"Butt out, Mother," she said without turning around.

"My daughter was taught basic social skills, Mitch. She's obviously tired and cranky—"

"And not twelve years old so you don't need to speak on my behalf, Mom." What was this, a conspiracy? She was getting tired of being ganged up on. "I mean it, Mitch. I don't appreciate this. I'm perfectly capable of unplugging a stopped up toilet by myself."

Instead of being angry, Mitch's lips twitched. He leaned against a pole and crossed his arms. "Oh, I'm sure you're a master at it. And you're welcome." Ignoring her, his gaze switched to her mother. "Are the kids here, Margaret?"

"In the back of the office, waiting anxiously for you."

"What?" Greta whirled to face her mother. "Waiting for what?"

"To go surfing again," Mitch said, causing Greta to do a one eighty yet again.

She was getting dizzy whirling around to glare at both her mother and at Mitch, so she backed up against the wall of the building to face them both.

"I see. How nice that you both planned my kids' day without consulting me."

Her mother crossed her arms. "Did you have something else organized for your children today?"

"Well, no. But that's not really the point, is it? They are *my* children."

"Yes, they are. And Mitch has offered to take them surfing again. Are you saying no?"

Dammit. She hated being cornered. If she kept the kids away from Mitch, she'd look petulant and childish. She had no good reason to deny Jeff and Zoey a fun day, and she knew they'd love to surf with him. She let out a resigned sigh. "They can go."

"Great," Mitch said, passing by Greta to throw his arm around her mother's shoulders. "Let's go get the kids."

Greta checked on the plumber, who unstopped her toilet in record time, replaced a worn out valve, then refused her offer of payment, saying Mitch had already taken care of the bill, much to her chagrin.

By the time she finished with the plumber and spent time in the office going over paperwork and paying bills, it was noon. She went in search of her mother, found her in the house packing a picnic basket.

"You going somewhere with that?" she asked.

"I'm not. You are."

Greta arched a brow. "Yeah? Where do you think I'm going?"

"You're going to put on your swimsuit, take this lunch out to share with Mitch and the kids, then spend the afternoon surfing."

"I am not."

Her mother put her hands on her hips, a signal she was digging in for battle. "Greta. You spend every damn day, twelve to fifteen hours of it, working. Do you think that's what your father had in mind for you when he left you this motel?"

How many times had they had this argument? "Dad knew I loved this place. I don't mind the work, Mom."

"Your life didn't end when Cody left, honey."

"I know that. My life doesn't feel over. I love what I'm doing."

"But you don't have fun anymore."

She resisted rolling her eyes. "I don't need to have fun. I need to be serious about making a living and raising my kids."

"That's a load of crap and you know it. Everyone is entitled to recreate. Your dad and I did plenty of it. He might have died too young, but we lived every moment of the lives we had together, with no regrets. Can you say the same about yourself?"

She hated seeing the tears in her mother's eyes, hated that she felt she brought them on. "My life is different than yours and Dad's."

"It doesn't have to be. I want to see you happy."

"I am happy."

Her mother inhaled, then sighed and spoke in a soft voice. "No, Greta. You're not, and haven't been for a very long time. But I think you can be." Her gaze drifted out to the surf, and Greta shook her head.

"With Mitch?" She shook her head. "Oh, Mom. You've got the wrong idea. We're just....having fun together."

"Are you? And that's all it is?"

"Yes."

"That was a quick answer."

"There's nothing between us."

Her mother came closer, grabbed her hands and held them. "I know you better than you know yourself sometimes, Greta Lynn. There's something between the two of you."

She laughed. "Yeah. He wants to buy the Crystal Sands and I don't want to sell it to him. That's what's between us."

Her mother cast a knowing smile her way. "If you say so."

"I say so. Trust me, we're just friends."

"Fine. But I'm here today and things are slow. Go surf and be a nice hostess to a man who's been showing you and your kids a good time."

Dammit. She hated when she lost a battle. "Fine."

Her mother handed her the picnic basket. "Good girl."

Twenty minutes later she was in her swimsuit, a coverup thrown over it, basket in hand and padding down the beach in search of Mitch and her kids. She paused as she found them tearing up the waves about a half mile down shore, marveling at her son's natural ability at surfing. He rode alone, high on top of a pretty good-sized wave, grin a mile wide as he cruised into the flat water, whooping for joy and grabbing his board to walk out of the surf. He waved as he spotted her.

Mitch was out in the water working with Zoey, paddling his board alongside hers, using infinite patience with her little girl who wasn't quite as sure-footed on a surfboard as her older brother.

Greta held her breath as Zoey caught the top of a smaller wave. Zoey balanced precariously, Mitch hollering instructions to her as he rode the same wave effortlessly, his gorgeous body at home on the crest as if he could ride it even without the board under his feet. Zoey bit her lip in concentration, and Greta knew how determined her daughter could be when she wanted to learn a new skill.

Greta didn't exhale until Zoey made the wave all the way into shore, and couldn't resist a tiny whoop of exclamation that she'd made it.

What would it be like to have more time to spend with her children, to watch them surf like this, to while away the hours recreating and just...enjoying life with them?

Maybe what Mitch offered wasn't such a bad idea after all. Maybe she was holding on to foolish dreams and it was time to think realistically. The things she could offer her children...

She couldn't imagine. She'd probably be bored. And the kids would become the idle rich. Bratty, spoiled, unappreciative of what they had. No, they were better off seeing what it was like to work hard for what they had in life. It had worked out okay for her.

"Did you see me, Mom?" Zoey asked as she ran up to her mother and threw her soaked body against Greta's waist.

"I did. You looked beautiful out there."

"Mitch has been teaching me balance."

Mitch came up just then, smiling, his wet hair slicked back, his tanned face absolutely gorgeous in the afternoon sun. He literally took her breath away, this forty-something surfer dude who could still grin like a teenager catching his first wave. "Mitch is very good at surfing."

"Aww, gee, thanks, Greta," he said with a wink.

She held up the basket. "My mother packed a picnic lunch."

"Awesome!" Jeff said. "I'm starving."

She rolled her eyes as Jeff grabbed the basket and he and Zoey went running toward one of the covered tables down the beach. "He's always starving. I fear another growth spurt coming on."

"He burns a lot of calories riding the board. He's a natural," Mitch said as they walked side by side down the beach.

"Like you always were when you were younger."

Mitch shrugged. "I had the drive in me. You could never drag me out of the water. But he wants something different."

Greta stopped. "He does?"

"So he says. He wants to be a marine biologist."

"He told you that?"

"Yeah. He's very concerned about environmental impact on sea life."

Holy shit. How could she not know this about her son? "I didn't know. He never said anything to me about this."

"It's all he talks about. He's incredibly knowledgeable about the topic for a kid his age."

An ache formed in the pit of her stomach, for many reasons. "I see."

She didn't say anything more because they'd reached the

table. Instead, she focused on actually having some time to spend with her kids that didn't involve directing them in chores for either the motel or the house. Though they weren't really interested in talking to her, instead focused on Mitch, on talking about surfing and rehashing what they'd managed to accomplish in a few days, which apparently had been a lot.

"They're both naturals in the water," Mitch told her, singing their praises. "They learn quick, they adapt and they listen to direction well."

Greta could see the kids beam under his praise. Coming from a world class surfer like Mitch, it meant something. "I appreciate you taking time to work with them. I know you're busy."

He shrugged. "I'm not busy at all. It's the holidays. And the kids are great."

Zoey grinned. "Mitch said I have great swimming ability, Mom. Maybe I can start up lessons again."

Mitch ruffled Zoey's hair. "It's good to have goals. And hey, if you start young like you are now, you might just yet meet your goal of making the Olympic swim team."

Her daughter wanted to be an Olympic swimmer? "Olympics?"

"Sure. I'm great at freestyle and backstroke. My instructor said so until we couldn't afford lessons anymore."

Guilt poured down on her like a brick building had fallen. "Yes. You've always been a great swimmer." She plastered on a smile until the kids were done with lunch, and had run off to do something nearby. Only then did she allow her façade to crumble.

"I had no idea," she said, staring into the bottled water. "Jeff wants to be a marine biologist and Zoey wants to be an Olympic swimmer. How could I not know these things about my own children?"

Mitch slid his hand under the table and squeezed hers. "Kids are always more open about their dreams to strangers than to their own parents."

She turned her gaze to his. "My children and I talk about everything. There are no secrets between us."

"They know how burdened you are with everyday life, Greta. They probably didn't want to add to it."

"Telling me their hopes and dreams isn't a burden."

"Isn't it? Knowing how you struggle to make ends meet, knowing what their dreams could potentially cost you? They're smart kids."

"I would do anything to give them what they wanted. College, a future, the Olympics." She pressed her fingers to her temples. How was she going to afford these things?

"Sell me the motel. Then you can give them everything they want. Everything you want."

Her head shot up. "That's what this is about? The motel?" She was agonizing about fulfilling her children's needs and he was angling it in a way that she would sell him the motel?

"No, that's not what this is about. But it's an answer."

Suddenly it hit her, a scenario so heinous it made her sick to her stomach. "You used them."

Mitch frowned. "What?"

"That's why they never mentioned marine biology and Olympics to me before."

"What are you talking about?"

"Those ideas were never in their heads until you put them there. How could you do that to them, Mitch? How could you set up my kids to further your own goals?"

He blanched, then reached for her hand. "Greta, I would never do that. They told me the first day on the beach about those things."

She jerked her hand away. "Bullshit." She slammed her chair back from the table and stood, so sick she palmed her stomach. "Pushing at me about the motel is one thing. I'm an adult. I can take it. But using my kids..." She glared at him. "Stay away from me. Stay away from my children."

He held up his hands. "Greta, you have it wrong. You know me. You have to know I would never use Jeff and Zoey that way."

She shook her head. "I don't believe you. I don't want to talk to you or see you again." Her eyes filled with tears and she blinked them back. "I mean it. You keep away from my kids. And you get the hell out of my motel. I want you out of there now." She left the picnic basket, ran to her kids to round them up and, despite their protests, hurried them back to the motel. Back to her home base, where she could protect them.

Where she could protect herself.

Where she could protect her heart from further being stomped on by a man she had thought she cared about, who she thought cared about her.

She changed clothes and locked herself in her office the rest of the day. Fortunately, her mother must have noticed how distraught she was, because she offered to take the kids with her. The kids were pretty upset by Mitch's abrupt departure, but she was doing what was best for them. They wouldn't understand how they could be manipulated by an adult.

She did, though.

She hadn't seen it coming, had been so overwhelmed by him, had let him lead her on, charm her children, her mother...

God, how could she be so stupid! It was one thing to use her—she'd had her eyes wide open the entire time. She knew what he wanted. She'd expected him to keep hammering away at her in his attempts to get her to sell the motel. But to prey on her children? That was unforgiveable.

She thought she knew him, thought she was getting to know him even better these last few days.

She didn't know him at all.

At least her ex-husband was up front about being a bastard. Mitch had been insidious about it.

When Heath came on duty early that evening, she let him take over and went to her house, took a shower and locked herself in for the night.

Tomorrow was Christmas Eve. She had things to do. She wasn't nearly ready for the holidays, and not even close to being in the holiday spirit.

She stared out the back door, watching the crest of white waves slide into the sand.

She thought of Mitch, of how easily he'd led her to believe he was a nice guy.

The things they'd done together...her body still burned remembering the way he'd touched her, kissed her, how it felt to have him inside her.

Her heart ached. She had started to care about Mitch, had started to think that maybe—

She wrapped her arms around herself, feeling stupid yet again.

When the hell was she going to smarten up about men? When was she going to learn that they couldn't be trusted?

When was she going to stop handing a man her heart on a silver platter so he could crush it in his hand?

Chapter Eleven

Mitch stood on the balcony of his penthouse suite in Daytona Beach, staring out at the blue water as dawn broke over the horizon.

For the first time in years, he didn't feel like grabbing a board and catching the first wave of the day. What he wanted to do was get in a car, drive down to Ft. Lincoln Beach and force Greta to listen to him.

He shouldn't have left. It wasn't like him to walk out on a fight, especially when he'd been unjustly accused. He should have stayed and talked to her, calmed her down, followed her back to the motel and made her listen to him until she believed him.

But Greta had been burned badly by a man before, so trust wasn't easy for her. Something about her kids, and their dreams, and her not knowing about them...

That wasn't territory he needed to be stomping all over.

He just hoped the Christmas present he'd left at her mother's house for the kids didn't piss her off. But he'd already done it and it was too late to undo it.

Eventually she'd figure everything out. Until then, the best thing he could do for her was stay the hell out of her way. She'd already had one man try to control her life. He wasn't going to be the next man to do it. She had to have the right to make some choices on her own.

He'd already made his choices, and he had some suggestions, if she'd ever give him the chance to tell her about them.

In a few days Greta had had a profound effect on him.

He sipped his coffee, looked out over the water and thought about the little girl with braces and braids he'd brushed off when he was an arrogant nineteen-year-old. He'd been destined for big things back then, couldn't wait to travel the world and see everything, make his fortune and become famous.

He'd traveled the world, seen everyone, made his fortune. Fame? Eh, he wasn't sure he was famous or not, or whether that even mattered.

The only thing that mattered to him right now was that little girl with braids and braces who'd grown into an amazingly capable woman with auburn hair and gorgeous emerald eyes. A woman who'd almost single handedly raised two bright, incredible children.

There was this family that he wanted to get to know better, because he cared about them. All of them.

Which frankly shocked the hell out of him, because if there was one thing Mitch Magruder didn't do, it was put down roots.

For the first time in his life, he suddenly wanted to. And that was a scary damn thing to even think about.

Unfortunately, the one person he wanted to talk to about it had just kicked him out of her life.

So now all he could do was take a step back and wait.

And hope.

Christmas Eve was always a bustle of activity for Greta. The kids, hyped up on excitement, drove her crazy, but always managed to drag her into the holiday spirit. And right now she really needed it after what had gone down with Mitch yesterday.

Jeff and Zoey had zoomed through their chores at the motel that day with vigor, knowing there was a payoff at the end of the day. She grinned watching them work, wondering why they couldn't be that zealous every day.

She had someone covering the motel that evening, so they headed off to her mother's for dinner. As was typical, the whole house was decked out in lights. Don had done most of the outside lights—beautiful white icicles that now draped down and blinked at passersby.

"Where's Mitch?" her mother asked as soon as they kids brushed by to go find their cousins.

"He's not coming, Mom."

Don frowned, leaning over their mother's shoulder. "Why not?"

Her mother crossed her arms. "I thought the two of you—"

"I don't want to talk about it. And don't mention it to the kids, either." She'd told Jeff and Zoey that Mitch had to leave on business at the last minute. They'd been disappointed, and of course it was a lie, but it was the best she could come up with. Now she could only hope her mother and brother would let the subject drop.

The tree was lit up, filled to maximum with ornaments, new and old, and the angel sitting at the top that Greta could still remember her father putting up there every year. It never failed to fill her eyes with tears seeing that burnished gold angel, tarnished with the passing years, sitting atop the sweet-smelling pine tree.

They ate ham and roast beef—turkey would come tomorrow—filled their bellies until they wanted to burst, then cleaned up and sat in the living room playing games and singing Christmas carols, laughing and reminiscing about holidays past. Don and Suz and their kids took off around eleven. They'd be back for lunch tomorrow. Jeff and Zoey headed into one of the bedrooms to watch a movie—hopefully to fall asleep—and Greta and her mother locked themselves in her mother's bedroom to do their annual midnight present wrapping.

"I swear, Mom," Greta said, dragging a bag onto the bed. "Every year I believe we're going to get to this early, and every year it seems to get later."

Her mother shrugged. "I already wrapped most of mine, so when I finish these last few I can help with yours."

"Thanks." Greta had bought clothes for the kids. Necessary evils and the kids hated it, but she also managed to save up for a new MP3 player for Jeff and some DVDs Zoey had put on her wish list. Had to put some fun things in there too.

"You want to talk to me about Mitch now?"

Greta shook her head. "He wasn't who I thought he was, that's all."

Her mother's fingers stalled on the gift she was wrapping. "What do you mean?"

"I really don't want to talk about this, Mom. Not right now." Not when her emotions were so raw. "Maybe after Christmas."

She heard her mother's sigh. "All right. But you know I'm always here for you, Greta."

"I know."

She went back to wrapping, trying to keep her head in thinking about tomorrow, about the looks on her kids faces when they opened their gifts. When the mattress bounced hard, her gaze shot up and she looked across the bed at a colorful, thick book her mother had plopped there.

"What's that?"

"A book for Jeff."

Greta laid her palms on the mattress and leaned forward to

read the title. Her heart started beating faster, her skin flushing with heat.

Colorful marine life littered the cover. The title of the book was spread out in sea-colored lettering: *World Wild Marine Life.*

"Mom?"

"Yeah."

Greta swallowed, her throat dry as a desert. "Why that book?"

"Jeff picked it up a few months ago when we were at the bookstore and was paging through it. Isn't it beautiful?"

Oh, God. Oh, God. Her legs wobbled and she sat on the side of the bed. "He did?"

"Yes. This one and several others about oceans and the environment. This one was the most expensive so I thought I'd get him this one to start, and maybe a couple others for his birthday in February."

Oh, shit.

"Greta, what's wrong? You look pale."

"Did you know Zoey wanted to be an Olympic Swimmer?"

Her mother laughed. "She swims like a fish, that one. Have you seen how long she can hold her breath under water, and how fast she swims laps at Don's pool?"

She'd seen Zoey swim before, but as usual her head had been on what needed to be done at the motel.

Where had she been when her children had needed her? When their dreams for the future had sprouted? Hadn't her eyes been open? Hadn't she been listening?

Where had she been when a wonderful man had tried to point these things out to her? Instead of recognizing this amazing gift, she'd thrown it back in his face and accused him of using her children to buy her motel.

She lifted her gaze to her mother. "Oh, Mom, I've made a

117

terrible mistake."

Her mother came over and sat on the bed next to her and took her hand. "Your palms are damp. What's wrong, honey?"

She explained about the beach, what Mitch had told her about the kids, then what she'd accused Mitch of doing.

Her mother frowned. "Greta. How could you think he'd use Jeff and Zoey that way?"

Her eyes stung with tears. She shook her head. "I don't know. Oh, Mom, I said awful things to him. My own inadequacies as a parent and I blamed them on him."

"That's enough. It's not your fault that you try to carry the weight of the world on your shoulders. If I hadn't been in the bookstore with Jeff and Zoey that day, I wouldn't have known about this, either. You know how kids are. They don't tell everyone everything, and often their friends know more about their dreams than their own parents."

Tears fell down her cheeks, her stomach clenching in pain and emptiness. What must Mitch think of her? "I feel so bad. For my kids, for Mitch. I've had my head so wrapped around that damn motel that I've neglected everything in my life."

"Now stop it. You have not. You're a good mother, Greta, and Jeff and Zoey love you. You give so much of yourself to them. Most kids would kill to have you for a mother."

She managed a smile. "Thanks, Mom. I appreciate that. But I need to stop living for that motel. I need to stop living for Dad." The last was said in a tiny voice, her gaze directed at her mother, hoping she wouldn't break her mother's heart.

But her mother's gaze never wavered. "It's about time you realized that. Greta, I have never interfered in the way you run the motel. Your father gave that to you to run as you please, and the decisions you make about it are yours."

"I know. But you know your input is always welcome."

"Well, I've never wanted to say anything, but I guess it's time I do. Greta, I loved your father with all that I have, all that I am. But he's gone. He will never be forgotten by any of us who loved him, but you don't honor his memory by refusing to live your own life. He wouldn't have wanted you to live in the past and never move forward. That's not why he left you the motel. He wouldn't want you to live frozen in the past. He wanted a future for you, honey."

She squeezed her eyes shut, realizing the mistakes she'd made because she was too afraid to take a step forward. She'd cocooned herself in her own little safe haven, and turned down the opportunity of a lifetime for herself, and more importantly, for her children.

She'd been so blind, in so many ways. "You're right." When she opened her eyes again, she knew exactly what she needed to do, where she needed to start. "I have to find Mitch. I need to apologize."

She went to her mother's computer and looked up the phone number for Mitch's hotel in Daytona Beach. He probably wasn't even there, had no doubt hopped a flight back to Hawaii. After all, why stay here now? But this was a start. She called the hotel, asked if Mitch was still there. They wouldn't give out that information, of course, but she asked the front desk to get him a message.

Now she could only hope his staff was as efficient as ever, and that her message would reach him.

She knew it was too late, that she'd lost the chance to be with the one man who'd given her hope. But she could at least tell him she was sorry.

"Greta, there's something I need to give you."

She looked up from the desk at her mother. "What?"

"Mitch brought this over the other day and asked that I keep it until Christmas morning, but you'd better take a look."

"What's in it?"

Her mother rolled her eyes. "I have no idea. The envelope is sealed."

It was a white envelope with her name on it. She took the envelope and slid her finger under the seal, opening it. Inside was a letter from some New York bank in official sounding language indicating that Mitch had set up a trust for Jeff and Zoey, with annual payouts to Greta for her children to take private swimming lessons. Trips for Jeff for marine research would be arranged at Greta's discretion, and their college education would be fully funded.

Under the letter, Mitch had hand written a note.

For your marine biologist and your Olympic swimmer. Merry Christmas, Greta. Love, Mitch.

Greta stopped breathing for a minute.

It wasn't an offer to buy the motel, there were no stipulations included. And when she'd sent him away, no second letter had arrived rescinding the trust.

Oh, Mitch.

Her heart ached so much she thought she'd die.

She handed the letter up to her mother, who read it, fell into the chair next to her and burst into tears.

Chapter Twelve

Greta did her best to hold it together Christmas Day, to be cheerful and fun for the kids, who loved all their gifts. They were always so appreciative of every gift they received, no matter how small.

Jeff loved his book on marine life, had found a quiet corner after all the chaos of present opening had died down to sift through every page. He sipped hot chocolate and read, seemingly content to be off by himself, not with his new MP3 player downloading tunes, but absorbing every page of the book.

Zoey was playing a new video game one of her cousins had received. Greta was inhaling her fourth cup of coffee since she hadn't managed to sleep last night. Neither her morning shower nor the caffeine seemed to be jolting her out of her zombie-like state.

Her brother wrapped his arm around her. "Stay up all night wrapping gifts?" he asked.

She managed a smile. "Something like that."

"You want to tell me what went down with you and Mitch? I warned him not to hurt you. If he did…"

She tilted her head back. "He didn't hurt me at all, Don. I hurt him."

Don frowned. "You know, I might be a big, dumb

fisherman, but I'm your brother and I'm here for you if you need to talk."

Her heart filled with warmth and love. She laid her head on his shoulder. "Thanks. I don't think you can help me, though. I really messed up."

He squeezed her harder. "There's nothing that can't be fixed, Greta."

If only. "This can't."

"Oh, I don't know about that. I'll bet it can."

She was about to argue, but Don half turned her, and she caught sight of the best Christmas present ever—her mother strolling down the hallway with Mitch at her side.

Her hand trembled, and Don took the cup away from her.

"Let me take that before you drop it and Mom yells at you," he whispered in her ear. "Merry Christmas, Mitch."

Mitch nodded at Don and smiled, but his gaze returned immediately to Greta.

"Mitch!" Jeff put the book down and launched off the chair, running to Mitch and throwing his arms around him. Mitch wrapped his arms around Jeff and hugged him tight.

"Hey Jeff! Merry Christmas."

Zoey came running in. "Mitch is here? Hi Mitch! Merry Christmas. Wait 'til you see all I got for Christmas." She hugged him and Mitch picked her up and hugged her back, closing his eyes tight as he did.

"Hey guys. I have gifts for you." He lifted a bag. "We'll open these in a bit. But first, I need to talk to your mom."

Greta felt the depth of his feeling for her children coming off him in waves. Her throat squeezed at the warmth and familial bond he already had with her kids. It was true and it was honest and she felt more like a jerk today than she had last night.

Greta's mother cleared her throat. "Let your mother talk to Mitch alone. You'll have plenty of time with him later. How about we go into the kitchen and eat some homemade biscuits?"

Distracted by food, the kids waved to Mitch, and the whole family eased out of the room.

And suddenly, the two of them were alone.

"Would you like to sit down?" she asked, feeling awkward, not knowing where to start.

"Sure." He moved to the sofa and sat.

She sat next to him, knowing she was going to have to make the first move, but suddenly tongue tied and nervous.

"I got your message last night," he started. "Thank you."

Her eyes welled with tears. "Mitch. I'm so sorry for everything I said. I was wrong—about a lot of things."

"Greta, it's okay."

She held up her hand. "It's not okay. Please, let me get this out before I end up falling apart."

"Okay."

"I was Daddy's little girl. We did everything together. He took care of me, was always there for me. And then Cody...well he took care of things, too, only he took it to the extreme. Then things got ugly with Cody, and Dad was there for me again to help me pick up the pieces. But he died right after that. So the motel was all I had left and I clung to that like it was the only thing important to me.

"I used the motel like a shrine to my father, the only man who had ever really meant anything to me, who had ever really loved me. And I see now how wrong that was, how much I've missed out on. Not only with my kids, but in life. And you're the one who opened my eyes to the things I could have. No monetary things, that kind of stuff never mattered to me. But time with my children, learning about who they are, what they want out of life. Just being able to be with them, enjoy life with them, before they're grown and gone.

"And also, time for me to be a woman, to fall in love again, to have time to myself to live. I had filed that part of myself away and that's not fair to me or to my kids. Thank you for letting me see glimpses of the woman I could be. I didn't even know she existed.

"I'll sell the motel to you, Mitch. But I don't want you to feel like you need to be part of our life. I just appreciate the time you spent with me, and with the kids. I'll never regret that."

She exhaled on a shaky sigh.

"Can I talk now?" he asked.

She nodded.

He slid his hand in hers, entwined his fingers with hers, and her gaze went down to where their hands were joined, then back up to meet his eyes.

"I have never been with a woman who wanted so little from me. All the women I've ever dated knew who I was, what I was worth, and what I could give them. I gave, and they took. Frankly, it was usually a mutually beneficial relationship. I had eye candy on my arm for whatever event I needed it for, and the women got whatever they wanted from me in return.

"I never did long term relationships because no woman wanted me just for me, and I didn't meet or was with any woman I was interested in getting to know better.

"Until you. You completely unraveled me and my expectations of what a woman wanted, because you didn't want a damn thing from me. Not my money, my connections, nothing. You asked for nothing, you expected nothing, and I had no idea what to do with someone like you, because instead of taking, you gave."

She frowned. "I don't understand. What did I give you?"

"Fun, warmth, laughter, family, heart, romance, sex, love. All without strings, without asking for anything in return. I've never in my life met a woman like you. And for the first time, I wondered what it would be like to...stay."

Greta swallowed...hard.

"I've never stayed before. I was always off on the next adventure, the next deal, never thinking twice about the woman I left behind, because there were never any strings.

"With you, Greta, there are strings. Not strings that you laid down, but the ones I've made. So, for the first time in my life, I find myself...attached." He dragged his fingers through his hair. "And I don't really know what the hell to do with all these feelings I have, because I've never had them before."

Greta lifted shaky fingers to his lips. "You've never been in love before, have you."

He shook his head. "No."

She smiled at the look of utter misery on his face. She could almost feel sorry for him if it wasn't so damned endearing, if he hadn't just laid his heart in her hands, if she didn't feel like bursting into tears she was so happy. "I thought I was in love once. But I was wrong. Love isn't giving and never receiving anything back. Love is when you give, and receive that same kind of feeling in return. Love is what I think I feel for you, Mitch."

He sucked in a breath and entwined his fingers with hers. "Is it possible to fall in love with someone after only a week?"

Her lips lifted. "I don't know. Maybe."

He squeezed her hands. "I will never hurt you like he did."

"I already know that. And I'm so sorry for ever thinking you could. That was my own hurt pride over not knowing my children as well as I thought I did."

"You don't have to sell me your motel."

She shook her head. "It's the right decision to make for me and for my kids."

He stared at her. "Then help me design it. And then help me run it."

Her heart leaped in her chest. "What?"

"You know this place better than me. You help me draw up the right plans for the resort. We'll work on it together. And then this will be your hotel, too. You'll run it."

"I don't know anything about running a resort."

He shrugged. "I didn't know anything about the hotel business before I bought my first one. Dive in and learn."

The thought of it scared the hell out of her, but excited her too. She could already envision the new hotel sitting on the sands right now. With a pool big enough for Zoey to swim laps in.

"You're already thinking, aren't you?"

She grinned. "Yes."

"Good."

But there was something else. "Mitch."

"Yeah?"

"That letter you left."

"Oh. Yeah."

"I didn't know about it when I called and left you that message. My mom brought it to me after I called you."

"Okay."

"I don't ever want you to think I did this because of the money you left my kids."

He smiled. "Greta, I've never met a woman who needed me less than you do. I would never think that."

She stood and took a few steps, then sat on his lap, twining her arms around his neck. "That's where you're wrong. I never realized how much I needed you until you were gone. But it has nothing to do with your money. I missed you."

He touched his forehead to hers, and when his gaze met hers again, there was a brightness in his eyes that she could swear were tears.

But big strong multimillionaires didn't cry, did they?

He cupped her cheeks and pressed his lips to hers, kissing her until her heart swelled so thick she was afraid it would burst from her chest.

"Merry Christmas, Greta."

She snuggled against him, realizing Mitch was undoubtedly the best Christmas gift she had ever received. "Merry Christmas, Mitch."

"Should we go tell the kids and your family all the news?"

She grinned, then nodded and stood, clasping tight to his hand. "Yes, let's definitely go tell everyone."

The kids were shocked, excited beyond words, and unable to believe their good fortune. They of course had to call all their friends and tell them the good news. Greta's mother just nodded, seemingly pleased. Don and Suz were elated and said they expected the royal treatment at the new hotel, which made Greta laugh.

They all ate and cleaned up, then everyone went home. Greta's mother insisted on keeping the kids overnight, and shooed Greta and Mitch out the door to go spend a night somewhere else.

Mitch drove them to Daytona Beach, back to his suite at his hotel. As they walked through the doors, Greta stepped out onto the balcony to breathe in the night air.

Mitch moved in behind her and wrapped his arms around her. "What are you thinking about?"

"Gifts."

"Yeah? What kind of gifts?"

"The kind that don't have anything to do with money or presents." She turned in his arms. "The kind that have to do with how a man and a woman feel about each other."

She leaned against him, pressed her lips against his to show him how she felt about him, wanting to give him the only gift she had to give.

His arms tightened around her and he deepened the kiss, his tongue wrapping around hers, coaxing her to open so he could lick against hers with velvet softness.

He moved his hand down to her lower back, his fingers resting just above her buttocks. He pressed in, driving her sex against his erection, letting her know how affected he was by their kissing. Greta clutched his arms, so lost in the sensations of the kiss that she didn't care that they stood on the balcony where anyone could see.

Then again, who could see? They were shut in on three sides, they were so high up someone would need binoculars, and if she walked him backward and pressed him up against the wall...

"Greta," he asked when she did just that. "What are you doing?"

She smiled, then slid down his body, enjoying the play of his muscles clenching in surprise. "Playing."

She'd worn her black dress today. Now, she hiked it up to her thighs, her legs spread as she crouched down, putting her face at level with his crotch. She unzipped his pants, tilting her head back to watch his reaction. His half-lidded gaze told her he wasn't going to object to her drawing his cock out right here on the balcony.

He hissed when she began to stroke it, then slid her lips over the soft head, capturing his salty essence with her tongue. He reached out one hand and slid it into her hair, winding his fingers around it to hold her head in place as she loved his cock with her mouth and tongue, holding the base of the shaft with her hand, taking as much of it in her mouth as she could.

She loved the sounds he made, the way he talked to her, encouraging her while she sucked him. Giving a man a blow job had never been such a turn-on before, had never aroused her as it did now. But Mitch was so into it, and she could tell she gave him pleasure, which made her want to give him more. She loved his groans, the way he pushed into her mouth, held on-to her hair with a tight grip as if he was holding back just so he could enjoy the pleasure.

She knew that feeling.

By the time he pulled his cock away from her lips, her nipples were hard and her pussy was quivering in anticipation. Mitch reached for her hands and lifted her.

"I want to come inside you, not in your mouth."

Panting with excitement, she kissed him, ravaging his tongue with hers, showing him just how out of control sucking him had made her.

He moved her to the edge of the balcony, placing her hands around the thick iron railing. He lifted her skirt, sliding his hands under the fabric to reach for her panties and slide them down her legs. Suddenly she felt the warm wetness of his tongue between her legs, and she widened her stance, giving him access. He slid one hand in front of her sex and found her clit, his tongue sliding up into her pussy and along her lips to drive her to near madness.

Soon she was on her toes, arching against his hand, so close to coming she had to bite down on her lip to keep the whimpers at bay. But just like him, she wanted to wait.

"Mitch. Fuck me. Now."

He pulled away, rose, and she heard the tearing of the condom packet. Then he was behind her, lifting her dress again, pushing her forward so her butt was in the air and his hand was on her ass, spreading her cheeks apart while his cock probed between her legs. Just the touch of his cock head against her pussy lips made her pulse, almost sent her over the edge.

"Mitch, please."

He thrust inside her, his hips buried against her ass. She tilted her head back and moaned at the sheer pleasure of this bond they shared, of feeling him connected to her in this intimate way. Her pussy gripped him, and he pulled back, the sensation of his cock dragging against her nerve endings near shattering her.

But she held on, not ready to come yet, wanting to enjoy every second of this joining.

Mitch bent forward, kissed her neck, licked her throat, then pushed her hair to the side and lightly bit her nape. She shivered, the wild sensation shooting between her legs and making her pussy clench his cock.

"Christ," he whispered, then reared back and thrust harder. "You do that again you're going to make me come."

She gripped the railing and pushed back, unable to speak, just needing more of what he'd just given her. More of the sweet hot pleasure of his cock impaling her. She released one of her hands and lifted her dress, found her clit, and rubbed.

"Oh, yeah," Mitch said. "I want to feel you come all over me."

His words, as dark as the night surrounding them, tightened her even further. With her hands and the measured pumps of his shaft, she splintered, waves of climax pouring over her, making her cry out into the night. She didn't care, the pleasure was too great. And Mitch went too, only adding to the wild sensation of abandon and primal release that filled the night as he gripped her hips and pumped hard once, twice, then shuddered against her, shouting too as he came before falling against her.

She couldn't recall ever having an orgasm that hard, that deep, one that left her drenched and sweaty and unable to move a muscle. Mitch wrapped an arm around her waist and turned her around to face him. He was wet too, perspiration dotting his forehead and neck.

"Ms. Mason, I do believe you are something of an exhibitionist and a wild thing."

She laughed. "Would you like me to add that to my resume, Mr. Magruder?"

He cocked a brow. "I don't think I want Human Resources to know that aspect of your...talents."

They stripped, took a shower and climbed into the fluffy bath robes provided by the hotel, then Mitch ordered room service snacks for them and they piled into the king-sized bed to eat and drink.

"Did you have a good Christmas, Greta?" he asked, feeding her a strawberry.

"I had an incredible Christmas, Mitch." The first that she could remember since her father died where she didn't go home and stand at the shore, look back at the motel and miss her dad. That was a very good sign that things were changing for the better. She'd like to think her father would like the decisions she was making. And he had always loved Mitch.

"So will you take off after the deal is made?" she asked.

Mitch frowned. "Why would I do that?"

She shrugged. "I just figured you had other business interests to occupy your time."

He took a sip of champagne, then set it on the table behind him. "You and Jeff and Zoey and the new resort will occupy my time. I intend to stay here, Greta."

"Oh." Hope swelled inside her.

"When I said I was falling in love with you, that didn't mean I was going to have a relationship with you long distance."

"Oh."

He picked up her hand and kissed her knuckles. "We need to see where this goes. You and me—it has nothing to do with the new resort. That's separate. Business and personal won't be mixing together."

"Can you do that?"

"Of course. Can you?"

"Yes. Though I will be sleeping with my boss. What will people think?"

He shook his head. "No, you will be sleeping with your partner. I intend to give you fifty percent equity in this resort, Greta."

Shock made her eyes widen. "Mitch. Why?"

"So you never feel like some man has control over you ever again. You and I will share equal interests and equal decision making in this resort. You won't ever report to me."

God, she really didn't deserve him. "Thank you for that."

"Don't thank me. You'll work your ass off for it."

"I'm not afraid of hard work."

"I already knew that. But it'll be awhile before the attorneys sort all the paperwork out, and we go through the permit stage. In the meantime, I intend to focus all my efforts on the personal aspects of our relationship."

She sighed as he drew her against him and pressed a long, toe-curling kiss to her lips.

She didn't know what she'd done to deserve a gift like Mitch, a man who'd swooped in and completely unraveled her life, but she could never go back to the way things were a week ago.

And why would she even want to? A week ago she was miserable. And every day since Mitch had shown up at her motel, she'd been falling hopelessly, helplessly in love.

It was the stuff of fairytales. She really did feel like Cinderella.

About the Author

Jaci Burton is a National Bestselling author, published in multiple genres. Her life is spent juggling deadlines and trying to keep the characters straight in all her books. Jaci is an award winning author, and has won the *Romantic Times Bookclub Magazine's* Reviewer's Choice Award. Jaci makes her home in northeast Oklahoma with her husband and more dogs than she can wrangle. You can find out more about Jaci and her books on the web at www.jaciburton.com

Look for these titles by
Jaci Burton

Now Available:

Rescue Me
Nothing Personal
Show Me
Unwrapped
Dare to Love
Unraveled

Print Anthologies
Holiday Seduction
Sneak Peek

Coming Soon:

Crimson Ties

Sweet Charity

Lauren Dane

Dedication

As always, this one is for my most awesome husband who makes this all possible and makes my life worth living simply by looking so good in a pair of jeans.

Thanks goes to Angie James, my fabulous editor, for always wanting to make me into a better author.

And to my readers, without whom none of this would be happening. Thank you for all your support.

Chapter One

The day wasn't too bad. Despite the fact that the air had a bite, the sky was clear and blue. She'd had a nice lunch, stopped by to see her mom on the way back to her shop and Christmas was coming. Not only was it a good time of year for her business but white and colored lights decorated the light posts and shop windows. Charity smiled with some amount of satisfaction because she'd nearly finished with all her shopping. Even better, she'd just found a gorgeous menorah to sit in the front window of her shop because Hanukkah was so close to Christmas this year she'd be able to celebrate both holidays at the same time. Nothing like feeling you'd checked off more items on the never-ending personal to-do list.

As she turned the corner to head back to her shop she caught sight of Gabriel Bettencourt leaning against his truck, all long and sexy. And her day just got even better. Mmm! Dark sunglasses shaded his eyes, and the beard and just-a-bit-too-long hair gave him an edge that thrilled everything right down to her toes. Charity's pulse sped as she took him in and pretended that *just friends* was just fine with her. Stupid pretending. All she really wanted to do was jump on him, knock him down and find out if that night eight years ago was a fluke.

She took her time approaching him, content to look her fill until he noticed her. Her fingers tightened on the lapels of the wool coat she wore, fighting against the always present desire to reach out and run her fingers through that black, shoulder-length hair.

He was dark and hot and she wanted to eat him with a spoon. Only, well it wasn't ever going to happen again and she needed to accept it. Someday anyway.

"Hey, Gabe, whatcha up to?" she said, sounding confident and nonchalant as she walked past.

"Charity." He reached up and removed the sunglasses, looking her up and down. At the blatantly sensual perusal her hormones threw a party. Man was she pathetic. A smile tipped the corner of his mouth. "Just waiting for my mom. She's picking up bread for the nine hundred relatives showing up for dinner tonight. What are you up to?"

She moved close to him out of a sheer perverse need to see if he'd react. They'd been playing this game for years now and at this point, Charity wasn't sure if it was real or all in her head.

"Coming back from lunch. Going to work now. Just took this way because I stopped in to say hello to my mom at the bank. And look at my reward for being a good daughter. I get to see tall, dark and delicious standing here in the winter sunshine." She winked, meaning it. "Oh, Gabriel, you should give all this up and run away with me."

He turned his head and they stood so very close. She drew in a deep breath, hoping for just a small touch but just barely missed. His eyes were brown, the color of dark chocolate and she knew that they went nearly black just after a kiss. Right then, they were pretty dark and she wondered if he'd kiss her. She doubted it. He never did.

"You wouldn't know what to do with me if you had me."

He said it like a joke but it really just made her mad. She took a step back. "I've had you, Gabriel, remember?" Moving back to the sidewalk, she gave him a glance over her shoulder. *Pig.* "I need to get back to work. Have fun with your bread."

She slammed back into the store and her assistant Faith—and yes, Faith and Charity, they got the joke so please don't ask where Hope is or someone will kick you—looked up, raising a brow.

"I don't know why I bother," Charity muttered, hanging her coat up.

"With what?" Faith asked, looking through some new stock that'd come in the day before. "Oh, nice." She held up a sweater and Charity nodded absently.

"Men."

"Shut up. God. There you stand all tall, dark and gorgeous and you talk that way. Pffft. Men love you."

"Sometimes." She shrugged. The truth was, the specter of that one, disastrous night with Gabriel eight years before haunted her. It wasn't like she hadn't had good sex since. Or she shouldn't say "since" because once they'd gotten naked it hadn't been good sex at all. Gabriel was all steamy and sexy and sort of dark and broody. She'd heard rumors of how hot and commanding he was in bed but with her? So very not.

Was it her? Had he been all into it and then saw her naked and wanted to run? He only went through the motions—stilted and totally unsatisfying motions—because he was already naked?

Gah. She should just stop thinking about it. There wasn't a damned thing to garner from this obsessive nitpicking of one experience she'd had eight years ago. There'd been four men between then and now and they'd all been very good in bed and had seemed to be into what she did. She *knew* she wasn't a dud in bed, but in her heart of hearts, she hated the idea that Gabe was horribly turned off by her when she was so hot for him. He ran hot and cold! Some days he would give her one of those sexy looks like he wanted to do her brains out and others he put all that into other women.

She'd have given up on him if she thought it was a game but Gabriel wasn't like that. Aside from all the sexual tension, they had a good friendship. She'd known him all her life and she liked him. More than that, she wanted him and had for more than just those eight years. Charity had wanted Gabriel Bettencourt for as long as she could remember. Having one small taste of him only made not having him hurt more.

Before she could discuss any of it with Faith, the store filled up with customers, it was coming up on Christmas after all and while many students from the university had gone home on break, there was a sizable local population out looking for holiday gifts and hot red sweaters to wear to impress recalcitrant men.

Hm. Charity's gaze snagged on the sweater Faith had pointed out earlier. Blood red and soft looking. Pair it with a skirt or some skinny black jeans and it could be an eye catcher.

Gabe watched her walk away and tried, by sheer will, to make his hard-on disappear before his mother returned. Ah, that did the trick. It was good to know thinking of his mom made his ardor cool.

Charity had *had* him alright and it had been one of the single most embarrassing few minutes of his life. Shit, he hadn't meant to make her mad or hurt her feelings with his retort. He'd been teasing, but poked into painful territory they never spoke of.

Still, Charity Harris looked damned good from behind, all long legs and high, tight ass. She'd looked even better naked, bearing the finest tits he'd ever laid eyes on outside a magazine. Acres of olive-toned skin and a mouth that made him stutter just thinking about it even eight years later.

She kissed like a goddess. Her lips were lush and soft, her tongue had been warm and wet and he knew from the way she'd licked at the inside of his mouth that she'd know what to do with it elsewhere, too.

He could still remember how her hair had felt against his chest as he'd rolled her over. And that's when it all went south.

He'd wanted her so damned badly and she'd been beneath him, naked and way more than willing and he'd given her a night about as hot as a fucking dental appointment. It had been so disastrous she'd hidden from him for the rest of that summer and went to UCLA without more than a waved goodbye.

Oh sure they'd patched it up over the time she would visit on weekends and during summers. They'd rebuilt a friendship over the years. He'd taken over operations at his family's dairy farm and she'd come back to Davis and opened up her successful second-hand and vintage clothing store near UC Davis. They were grownups now and both had full lives and all that jazz.

But always between them, the sexual tension simmered and he still wanted her so badly his teeth hurt. He'd *always* wanted her, wanted her right then as she'd stood just a breath away from him. But she wasn't for him and he knew it.

Charity Harris was a nice, sexy woman but he liked sex rough and hard. It was holding back that night eight years ago that had created the problem. Charity was sweet. The kind of woman who liked candlelight not candlewax. He cared too much about her to do things she'd hate or, worse, things that would scare her and make her think less of him. The thought of not having her in his life at all, of having her be repulsed by him kept his hands away from that luscious body. He valued their friendship enough that he couldn't stand to ruin it by pursuing her and both of them being unhappy.

No. He'd laugh with her and flirt a bit and find his entertainment elsewhere. She'd find herself a nice guy like his brother Rafe or one of his sister-in-law's male siblings who oozed all that gallantry the women seemed to go wild for.

143

Eventually his feelings for her would mellow out, he'd find the woman who could submit to him and still be an equal and this crush would be a fond memory.

Chapter Two

"Wow, that's some sweater." Belle Bettencourt, one of Charity's oldest friends who also happened to be Gabriel's sister-in-law, looked her up and down as she approached the table and sat down.

"Thanks. It came through the shop a few days ago and I had to have it."

"Well it shows off your, um, assets quite well."

Charity laughed. "Good. That's what I was aiming for."

The waiter came by and Charity looked at Belle for a moment before leaning forward and happily taking in the way the waiter's eyes widened at the sight of the soft, tight, blood red sweater with the keyhole opening at the neck. She took in his nametag, this was a college student job so they tended to be interchangeable over the years. "Hey there, Scott. I'd like two shots of Cuervo, don't forget the lime, salt and two Coronas."

Belle laughed and sat back. "It's like that?"

Charity turned to her friend and caught sight of Gabriel in one of the back booths with Rafe and Belle's oldest brother, Brian. She waved and noticed the way Gabriel homed in on that sweater for a moment before waving back.

"Ah, it all becomes clear now," Belle said archly. "This is about Gabriel."

Charity shrugged. "There are moments when he looks at

me like he wants to lick me up one side and down the other and others when he runs the other way. Always some damned woman on his arm. Christ, Belle, not to be vain or anything, but I'm hot! What is his deal?"

Scott the waiter brought the shots and the Coronas.

"Wait there a sec, Scott." Charity held her eyes on Gabriel, licked the side of her hand, shook out the salt, licked her skin again, took the shot and sucked the lime. "I'm going to need another one of those."

Scott ran off to obey and she smiled at Belle, who carefully wiped the outside of the lime and shook the salt into the shot instead of on her hand. After she took the shot, she sighed happily. "Hits the spot. I've been in court twice this week, had to file more motions than normal and I'm tired. However, I need to eat if I'm going to keep up with you."

More shots appeared and she fluttered her lashes up at Scott. "Scott, Belle and I need food to go with our drinks." She ordered a burger and fries, not caring about the calories for the moment, and Belle did the same.

"So back to the Gabriel thing. Yes, of course you're hot." Belle waved a hand. "I don't know what the deal is with him. Why have *you* waited all this time? Why not just go for it?"

Charity sighed and sipped her beer. Scott showed up with two more shots and some fries to "tide them over" until their orders came.

"First I waited to see if it would go away. Believe me when I tell you this, Belle, but the one time we had sex it was not memorable for any other reason but sheer awfulness. So you know, I went off to school and came back on breaks and stuff and he was still here and eventually we were able to be friends again. He was with other women, I was with other men. I thought maybe it was better to just let it go. But this thing between us never went away. I used to wonder if I imagined it but I see the way he watched me take a shot just now. He's interested but he holds back and I don't know why. I know he's not gay, or at least not all the way."

Belle laughed and they attacked their burgers with gusto once they arrived. Or rather, Charity ate hers like a Hoover vacuum and Belle used a knife and fork. But Belle was like that and Charity loved her anyway.

"He might be bi, I'm not with him every moment of the day or anything. But he likes girls. I know that, anyone with eyes knows that." Belle dabbed her lips with the napkin.

They both laughed.

"So why not me?" With an annoyed groan, Charity stood. "Jukebox. Any requests?"

"Something good to sway to when you walk back here."

"Belle, you're awesome."

She walked past the booths, waving at Gabriel, Rafe and Brian. The jukebox was filled with everything from Conway Twitty to Massive Attack. She fed it quarters and chose, smiling and bouncing past Gabriel again as Marvin Gaye and Tammi Terrell started to sing "Ain't No Mountain".

"Oh, good choice." Belle laughed as Charity sat back down. "Gabe's eyes were glued to your boobs and then when you passed them, your ass."

"I don't want his eyes on me, I want his hands on me."

More shots arrived and she laughed as she took it. Belle waved it away.

"Rafe is already looking at me with that gleam in his eyes."

"Rafe is eleventy kinds of sexy. You two are so good with each other." She smiled, happy for her friends but damn it, wanting it for herself, too.

Belle blushed. "Rafe *is* all kinds of sexy, isn't he? Just confront him! Gabriel that is. Go over there and ask him what his deal is. What do you have to lose? I mooned over Rafe for years and wham, suddenly he was kissing me! I've never been happier. You've had this thing for Gabriel since we were in high school. What if now is the time? What if, you know, you and Gabe could have what Rafe and I do?"

"Why don't you put us all out of misery and fuck the woman?" Rafe asked Gabriel.

"What? Who?" He'd been staring so hard at Charity he'd only halfway heard the question. He turned to Rafe and Brian and exhaled sharply.

Brian laughed. "Charity Harris. You know, the woman you told me two years ago that if I ever touched or tried to get naked you'd kill me and bury my body where no one would find it? The woman you've been staring at all night? All that licking business is making me wonder about my chances at being murdered by you. I do so love all that long, curvy stuff she's got under her clothes. Why you two sniff around each other but never do anything about is beyond me. It's also a waste of a very hot woman."

Who *wasn't* staring at her in that sweater? Her sable-dark hair loose around her shoulders, lips as red as the sweater. Her tongue, each time she took a shot, and it had been four now, darting out to lick her hand, God, the sight had been enough to make him whimper.

He focused his eyes again to glare at Brian. "She's a friend. You're a hound. Of course I warned you off." Even Gabe didn't believe himself. He supposed if he hadn't lost his voice twice in one sentence it might be more convincing.

"Hi."

He looked up, and up some more past the breasts heaving from the front of the sweater, past the hair and up into those green eyes of hers. *Zing.* Their connection shot straight to his toes. And um, other parts.

"Hey, Charity, you and Jose Cuervo having a good time?" *Keep it light.*

She plopped herself in his lap and his arms went around her to keep them both from falling. So much for that. "Gabriel, why don't you find me fuckable? What? Am I ugly? Fat? Do I smell? Did I make a weird noise before? Why do you run from me?"

"I'm going to check on Belle. You know, to see if she wants a ride home," Rafe said, shoving at Brian who stared at the mouthwatering tits currently pressed against Gabe's chest.

Gabriel wanted to throttle his friend for looking at her that way and didn't truly relax until the other two guys had gone and he and Charity were left alone. Although relaxed wasn't exactly what he felt just then.

Her lips just touched his ear, her breath against the sensitive skin. "Now that we're alone, you can tell me. It drives me crazy, you know. Why don't you want me?" She nuzzled into his neck and he stifled a groan.

"Honey, you're drunk." He knew it from the way she spoke. He'd heard her say the "f" word maybe a handful of times in the years he'd known her. She was also clearly out of it not to feel the rock hard cock she'd planted her sweet ass on.

"I am drunk, yes. If I wasn't, I'd be pretending that night eight years ago never happened. I'd be pretending it doesn't bother me that you didn't make me come. That I ran off and then we didn't talk to each other for nearly a year and now we circle each other and I think you're interested but other times you couldn't be less interested. It makes me very frustrated and there's only so much masturbating I can do and now apparently you've been warning men away. Tsk tsk, Gabriel. Brian might be the guy to give me what I need. Why so interested in telling him to back off?"

He tried not to smile. She was drunk and slurring her words slightly but she was on a mission and this was the woman he'd known for nearly thirty years demanding an answer. She was damned cute although squirming a lot, which wasn't helping his cock or his resolve to keep away from her.

Rafe approached, one of his eyebrows rising as he caught sight of how low Gabriel's hand rested on Charity's back, just above the sweet curve of her ass. "I'm going to take Belle home. She's very fun when she's been taking tequila shots. Thanks for that, Charity." He winked and Charity laughed.

"Merry Christmas from me to you."

Gabriel stood, bringing Charity to her feet but keeping an arm around her waist. "I'm going to take you home. You can't drive like this."

"I can take her," Brian said, wearing a smirk.

"I've got it." Gabriel glared and walked her out.

"I'm fine. I can get a ride with someone else since you hate being with me so much."

Gabe leaned her against his truck until he got it unlocked and opened. "Get in and stop that now. You know that's bullshit."

She snorted but got in, swinging those long legs inside.

He walked around, taking a deep breath of the cold air and praying for strength. He hated that she'd think he felt she was unattractive. Especially when the opposite was true. Eight years ago was not her fault.

"You're not going to puke in my truck are you?" he asked, starting the truck and putting his seatbelt on.

She rolled her eyes. "I'm not some college dumbass who can't hold her liquor. I only had four shots and we both know I'm capable of keeping up with you on that score. I wouldn't drive just now, but I'm not gonna puke."

"Just checking. Don't get pissy with me. You're at that new townhouse complex now right?"

"Yes. I'll get pissy if I want to. And you haven't answered my questions."

"Because they're stupid questions. We were kids eight years ago and you know damned good and well you're a beautiful, sexy woman."

She crossed her arms over her chest and fumed the rest of the way to her house, which was fine with him.

"Take this lane here on the left. I'm the last driveway on the end."

He pulled up, turning the truck off. He turned to speak but she practically leapt at him, throwing her arms around his neck, pressing her breasts against his chest and her mouth to his.

It was over for his self control as those lips of hers touched his. Within moments he was out of his seatbelt and his hands were in her hair. That soft, beautiful hair he wanted to wrap around his fist.

He let himself kiss her, let himself marvel at her taste when his tongue slipped into her mouth. She moaned, pressing against him more confidently, tossing her leg over his body and straddling his lap.

White bursts of light pinpricked against his closed eyelids as she ground herself over his cock and it was his turn to groan.

Firmly but not as hard as he really wanted, he pulled her hair enough to break the kiss. He'd intended to get out and drag her inside and run the other way but her neck was too tempting. Instead, he angled her the way he wanted. He feasted on her frantic pulsebeat just beneath her ear before cruising down the column of her throat where she was warm and smelled damned good.

The edge of his teeth tested the skin at the hollow of her throat and she moaned, arching into him. Her fingers pulled his hair, keeping him close.

The sound of a car door closing somewhere else on the small lane broke into his brain, and he grabbed her by the waist and set her on the seat again as he tried to catch his breath.

"Christ."

"Come inside with me." Her eyes were bright and clear but she was still under the influence of four shots of tequila and there was no way he'd have sex with a woman who'd had that much to drink.

Still, he wanted to get her inside safely so he helped her out of the truck and walked her to the door.

The place was nice. He hadn't been inside it, having been away the weekend she'd moved a few months back. It smelled like her, spicy, like cinnamon.

"Where's your bedroom?"

She smiled up at him, sliding her palm up his chest. "Up the stairs and to the left."

He helped her up and then saw the doors to her bedroom standing open. Her bed was covered in a big, fluffy comforter and lots of pillows. The room was more girly than he'd figured it would be and *Christ*, her panty drawer was open and heaps of lacy, frilly, brightly colored lingerie boiled up and over the edges like a sex explosion.

He imagined what her ass would look like in those boyshorts, her cheeks peeking out the bottom. Maybe pinked from his hand.

No. Not now.

She fell to the bed, kicking her shoes off.

"All right, well I'm gonna go now. I'll see you soon."

She sat up and pulled her sweater off and his mouth dried up at the sight of her breasts in a delicious bra the same red as the sweater had been. He froze in the doorway, watching her shimmy out of her jeans. The thong was the same color as the bra.

"You are not going to leave right now." She fell back to the bed. "If you leave I will hunt you down and kill you."

"Charity, you're drunk. I don't fuck drunk women." He held onto the door, his knuckles going white to keep from moving to her. "It's not right."

She opened her thighs and slid her hand down the front of her panties. "Gabriel, if it's wrong, I don't want to be right. Come on, I'm not some random woman you picked up at a bar. You know I'm consenting. You know I'd want you any other day too. I'm so wet." She made a sound in the back of her throat and he stumbled back into the hallway. "I need you." Her voice tore at him, pulled at him, desire thick. He could see her fingers moving against her pussy through the sheer material of her thong.

He swallowed hard, trying not to whimper at how much he wanted her, how much he wanted to go to her right then and ease her. That want had lodged in his gut since he was seventeen and it hadn't ever let go.

"Don't do this. We'll talk later. I'm going to lock up behind myself. Drink some water." He considered taking her some, but holy baby Santa Claus and his reindeer, he wanted to pull the hand from the front of her panties and suck her fingers into his mouth before pressing his face to her cunt.

Nope, not enough control to go in there.

"I'm going now. Get some sleep," he called out.

"You're leaving without making me come again, Gabriel. You suck."

He laughed without humor and left, each step a new lesson

in pain from how hard he was.

Chapter Three

The birds singing outside her window woke Charity up slowly. Her hand was still down the front of her panties and she groaned, remembering how horny she'd been and how Gabriel had walked out on her.

She couldn't help but groan as she got out of bed and shuffled to the bathroom, turning on the water for a shower. A clear head was needed to puzzle over what to do next and a shower would hopefully do the trick.

As she washed her hair and waited for the pain relievers she took to work, she worked up a head of steam just thinking about the night before.

First of all, hello, the kiss he had laid on her was *not* the same as before. The kiss last night was hot and hard and sort of dark. She might have been tipsy but she remembered the way he'd yanked on her hair to kiss her neck, the way his hands had trembled as she ground herself over his cock.

All right, she could admit it, she had some major league feelings for Gabriel. Last night had let them surge through her, past the wall she'd built over the years. There was simply no more denying it.

He'd wanted her enough to let himself kiss her for real in his truck and yet, he'd walked away. She'd had on her sexiest undies and even started to masturbate in front of him and he left! What was the deal?

That whole "we'll talk later" crap made her grind her teeth as she slapped on lotion and wandered into her bedroom to get clothes.

Charity wanted some answers, and she'd have them! She pulled on a pair of eggplant toned boyshort panties and the matching bra before getting socks and jeans on. Since she knew he'd be at the dairy she pulled on her boots and found a purple sweater with a cowl neck.

This was a war and Charity Harris meant to win it. To do so, she'd have to swallow her pride and use every weapon she had. First, her looks and her body. She had to do everything just right so she did her hair, making it full with big curls. Just the perfect amount of makeup, Gabe was a farm boy at heart, she'd seen him with super glammed-up girls before, but she knew he liked natural beauty so she'd go with that.

Gabriel Bettencourt was what she wanted. Had wanted for years now and all this pussyfooting around was for suckers. She was getting older, she wanted to settle down and start her life with someone. She had a house and a business and a lovely family, having a partner was the next logical step. Gabriel was going to be that partner unless he could give her a logical reason why not.

She got into her car and headed over to the Bettencourt Family Dairy about fifteen minutes away from her place. Where the city wore away and the country began to take over.

Her parents lived out this way, in the house she and her siblings grew up in. Her grandparents lived about three miles from her parents and they all had a big family dinner every other Sunday. It was pretty old school but Charity felt lucky at having all her family so close.

While she thought of it, she made a mental note to stop in at her grandparents' on her way back home. She'd seen her granny for lunch a week back but she liked to keep an eye on them.

Family was important to Charity, which was one of the many reasons she liked Gabriel. He worked at the family business, he took care of his mother, made sure his father didn't overdo it but always felt integral to the operations of their business. Family was important to him, too. She liked that in a man.

Priorities were central to any successful life and she didn't want to be with someone who didn't care about the things she did. Plus he was Portuguese like her mother. In fact, Charity's mom and Beatriz, Gabriel's mom, were good friends and often worked together on planning *festas*. Rosemary, Gabe and Rafe's sister, had been on the *festa* court along with Charity and they remained close friends to that day. Over Charity's life, she'd spent a great deal of time with the Bettencourts. They were like her extended family. She enjoyed being with them.

Despite her annoyance, she still felt lighter for admitting her feelings to herself as she took her left turn. The Bettencourt's house sat on an acre or so just to the south of the actual dairy farm. They had a little retail storefront there as well as a new milk delivery service Raphael had come up with, along with delivery from some of the other local businesses. Fresh fruits, nuts and veggies were available as well.

She pulled up and got out, having long since become accustomed to the smell of cows and cow shit. The presence of a world class university didn't mean Davis wasn't still a small town at heart. She saw Beatriz Bettencourt, Gabriel's mother, behind the counter and waved as she came through the door. The woman was in her late fifties and still looked amazing.

"Morning, Mrs. Bettencourt! I'm looking for Gabriel, is he around?"

Beatriz smiled as she gave Charity the once over. Sly but knowing, that face. Lucky for Charity, Mrs. Bettencourt liked her and if she thought a romance between Charity and Gabriel was a good thing, she'd be a solid ally. Hmpf, he thought he was so smart. Not so much there, boyo. Yet another weapon in her arsenal. Gabriel Bettencourt was going down.

"He seemed agitated this morning so he went for a ride. Would that mood have anything to do with you?"

Charity rolled her eyes. "He's very stubborn."

Beatriz laughed. "He is. So are you. That's good. He'd run right over any woman who wasn't as strong as he was. I know it's been a while, but I remember you riding horses in all the *festa* parades. Go on, you know where the stable is."

Charity smiled and gave the other woman a kiss on both cheeks. "*Obrigado.*" She thanked Beatriz and grabbed her coat from the car before heading to the stable.

Beatriz must have called ahead because one of the hands had a horse ready to go when she arrived and she swung up and into the saddle, getting herself familiar with the horse and her lead before they set out.

Charity hadn't ridden in two years but she'd done enough as a child and into her young adulthood that it wasn't hard to find her seat again.

"Last I saw Gabriel, he was out east," the hand said as he pointed northeast toward a copse of trees off in the far distance.

"Thanks!" she called and rode in that direction.

It was a good ride, enough time to gather her thoughts, work on her mad and at least the cold air helped with her headache.

The Bettencourts' land was larger than it appeared. The dairy sat on the southern acres but out to the north it was farmland they leased and past that, wilder land that hugged the riverbed.

The air was clean, fresh, the wind blowing opposite the dairy so all she smelled was earth and water and green from the trees. Sometimes being in town so much she tended to forget this part of Davis was so wonderful even though she saw it as she drove past. This was the part of her life she missed and coincidentally, it was the part of Davis Gabe existed in most often. Rugged, earthy, a place where men and women worked long hard hours to bring the rest of the world the things they needed. Charity had always found farming noble but not exotic like most of her classmates and friends back in LA did. Men like Gabe were different from the boys she dated in college, from the ones she dated here in Davis even.

There was a wildness in him, at the same time a sturdy reliability, a sort of steadfastness she found incredibly alluring. Gabriel Bettencourt was the kind of man who *did* things. He made things happen. A silly thought flitted through her head about camping with him. He'd be one of those guys who'd frown on bringing a truck full of gear. He'd make fires and cook fish he caught that day over them. He'd probably look really good naked in the starlight too.

But for the moment, she had bigger fish of the tall, dark and very handsome persuasion to fry. One who looked remarkably good with his denim jacket lined in wool, faded jeans and scuffed boots. The modern touch of a wool watch cap only made him more sexy.

It couldn't be. Gabe heard her voice, calling his name. He needed to have sex or something. Aural hallucinations were clearly a symptom of his useless obsession with Charity.

"Gabriel David Bettencourt, wait up!"

He reined his horse around and faced what was a lot more like an angry goddess than a hallucination. She rode toward him, her hair flying away from her gorgeous face, her legs encased in dark denim. She looked natural there seated on the mare but also exotic with her perfectly manicured nails.

"What are you doing here?" he asked, hoping he didn't

sound as lovesick as he felt.

"Nice to see you, too," she snapped, those green eyes flashing. "I'm here because you ran out on me last night."

"I'm surprised you remember any of it. I didn't run out on you. I dumped your drunk ass in bed and went home like a gentleman."

"Gentleman! Bah!"

He nearly laughed but wisely decided she might try to hurt him if he did.

"Are you insinuating I wasn't a gentleman?"

"First of all, did I ask you to be a gentleman? If I recall, I asked you to have sex with me. I don't want you to be a gentleman. Why are you so obsessed with that on my account anyway? When have I asked you to be anything but genuine?"

"So I'm not genuinely gentlemanly?"

"Gabe! I am going to kick you in the wedding tackle if you don't stop being so obtuse. What is the issue? Seriously. This thing has been between us for years. I know I'm not imagining it. I know you kissed me back last night and I sure as hell know it was different than it's been before. It was *hot*. You grabbed my hair, you gave me all I wanted and more. How can you be like that one minute and act like I'm stinkier than a cow patty the next? You're giving me a complex. Am I horrible? Was that your pity kiss?"

"What on earth would make you think you were horrible? Charity, you're beautiful. You know that. You're constantly being chased around by men all over Davis." He hated the look on her face.

"Are you my friend?"

He jerked back. "Of course I am. We've been friends since third grade."

"Then why are you dodging my questions? Come on. Give

me a break. I've been chasing you and chasing you and it's humiliating now. Put me out of my misery if that's the case. If you don't find me attractive just say so. Then I can lick my wounds and in a few months we can be friends again, sans the flirting. Because, Gabe, I am crushing on you in a major way. I have been for a very long time. Please. Just tell me."

She'd been so bold to come out here and tell him all this stuff, he had to be honest. And the knowledge she'd been yearning for him as much as he had her drove him to clamp down on the smile he wanted to give her.

"Yes, okay? I am attracted to you. A man would have to be blind not to be attracted to you. But we're friends and I don't want to ruin that."

The soft look on her face slid away into annoyance. "*Friends*! You just want to be friends? Why did you kiss me back last night then? You want to have sex with me, just admit it, you big wimp. I came out here, I'm being totally honest and you're dancing around like a lawyer instead of a dairy farmer. Let Belle do the lawyering, bucko, she's good at it. Give. Me. A. Straight. Answer."

He scrubbed his hands over his face. "You're a pain in the ass. I kissed you because I want to kiss you every time I see you and yes, I want to fuck you, too. But it doesn't mean we should."

"We need to discuss this mess. You're coming to dinner at my house tonight. Seven. Don't be late." She turned her horse around and rode off, leaving him behind, his mouth still hanging open.

Chapter Four

Dinner. She'd made it thousands of times. Had made it for men dozens of times so why did she feel like such a moron? Charity browsed through the racks of clothing in her shop, looking for something new to wear that night for dinner with Gabriel.

"Charity, I've seen you snare more than one male. Why let this one be any different? Come on, I really think you need to tell me the whole story. I've been begging you for years now," Faith said.

She looked up at her friend and sighed. Why not just tell it? "Because this one *is* different. The whatever-it-is between me and Gabriel goes way back. When I was like, oh, sixteen I think, he was seventeen, we were off doing something, can't remember why but I'm sure we weren't supposed to be doing it. We were down at the river. It had been hot and we'd been using a tire swing. You know, out over the water, you jump off, whatever.

"We'd been there hours and hours, laughing, playing. About twenty of us. And suddenly he just looked at me. We'd been joking and suddenly it was like he *saw* me. Really saw me as a girl and everything. It started then."

Faith leaned in, grinning. "How romantic!"

"Okay so I sort of said Gabriel and I had a brief thing and I went to college. It goes like this. He was a year ahead in school and I'd just graduated. I was due to head off to UCLA in the fall but I had all summer to hang out and just have a good time. He had his own place with Rafe, this house out on Bettencourt land actually. There was a party out there pretty much every other night. For a few parties running he and I had had this major chemistry. He'd kissed me at one of them. Nothing super sexual or anything, but it was all simmering beneath the surface."

"Oh the best kind!" Faith grinned.

"Yep. Anyway, so I came out there and it was late. We'd all been swimming and had come back and I don't know, I was in his room all the sudden and we were kissing. It was the hottest thing. No guy in high school had *ever* kissed me that way. In fact, until he kissed me again last night, no one had kissed me that way since. That kiss owned me. I wanted him so much. One thing led to another but somewhere along the line it just turned...*awkward*. Uncomfortable. When he was done he just sort of rolled over and apologized." Charity cringed at the memory and Faith made a sympathetic face.

"Anyway, it was horrible. The single worst sexual experience of my life. I ran out of there and avoided him and all those parties for the rest of the summer and went away to school. I really didn't talk to him again until I was in my second year and we didn't really reconnect our friendship until I'd graduated and come back to Davis. We've been friends a long time, I wouldn't want to lose it. But I think we can be more." She wanted so much more.

"Oh my God, what a horrible story. Ack! Did he ever tell you what happened?"

"Not really. When I moved back here, we just sort of pretended it never happened. I've never confronted it directly until last night. I'm gonna know just what his problem is if it kills us both." She paused. "Faith, I really like Gabriel. *Like* him like him."

"Well then take him." Faith shrugged, not doubting

Charity's ability for a moment and it cheered her immensely.

She pulled a dress from the rack and looked it over slowly. It had potential

A pair of mary jane heels with stockings and a garter belt would complete the look. Assuming she could get him to peel away the layers to get that far.

A week until Christmas so they'd be crazy busy until the 23rd when they'd close early and then stay closed until the day after Christmas. The store was packed all day and Charity knew she'd be able to give Faith a nice bonus based on her profits.

Her mother and sister came through the door in the early afternoon with coffee and scones.

"Thought you might need a pick-me-up. Looks like a busy day for you, huh?" Her mother kissed her cheek and picked up a scarf Charity had actually laid aside to give her mother for her birthday in January. "Pretty. I'll take it."

"Mom, you were just in here two days ago." Charity grinned at her sister, Marta, over their mom's shoulder.

"I know but you get new stuff in all the time. What if I miss something good like this scarf?" Paula Harris was the source of Charity's love of clothing. When Charity and Marta were young, they'd go out with their mom, their Grandma Dores, their Aunt Carmen and their cousins, and they'd hit garage sales and second-hand stores once a month. As a group, they still managed to get out once every few months even though her grandmother wasn't as spry as she used to be.

Charity could spot vintage across a room in the back of a rack or folded up and forgotten on a shelf of a junk shop. Her mother had bred a second sense into her and because of that, she had some gorgeous pieces in her closet she'd never have been able to afford without flea markets and thrift stores.

Charity's shop, Second Time Around, wasn't a junk shop or

a thrift shop. She was very choosy about what she took in, many items on consignment. She also hit her share of garage sales, flea markets and estate sales to find stock. As such, she'd built a unique business for herself and had created a solid profile in town. She was proud of what she'd done *and* that she'd done it in her home town. It was nice that half her customers were family or friends of her family. Coming from a big extended family had many plusses.

"Mom, if you come in here every other day, I'll never be able to give you any of my stock for presents unless I hide it all before I open the doors." She winked and her mom laughed.

"You coming to dinner tonight?" her mother asked while Charity rang up another customer and wished them a good day. "We'll have a full house. Jeremy gets back this afternoon, your cousins are gathering over at Carmen's. Jason is bringing his new girlfriend, whatsterface."

Poor woman wouldn't last a week once her mother started in on the whatsherface thing. Gina seemed nice enough but according to her mother, had a "horseface" and bad manners.

"I have a date."

Her mother's gaze sharpened and Marta laughed. "Who?"

"Gabriel is coming to dinner. I'll stop by the house on my way home to say hey and I'll be over for brunch tomorrow."

She tried to act casual but her mother had had her eyes on the Bettencourt boys for her girls forever and a day. She'd even joked about it with Belle's mother when Rafe and Belle got married earlier that year.

"Do you need any help?"

Charity laughed. "I'm capable of making dinner, thank you."

"It's about time. Invite him to brunch tomorrow." Her mother nodded like it was a done deal. Charity wished she had her mom's confidence. Gabe was wily.

"We'll see. Now go. I'll stop by on my way home."

"Okay. Love you."

"You're in for it now. You know she's going to send you home with half a pig and a cake too," Marta murmured as she hugged her sister.

Her parents' house was definitely full when she came through the front door. Jeremy, her baby brother, was getting his Doctor of Veterinary Medicine degree right there in Davis but he'd been at a conference in Oregon and had just returned that day. He was tall and fair like their father although he shared the green eyes the sisters and their mother had.

"Hear you have a date with Gabe," he said without preamble as she hugged him.

"Jeebus the gossip mill in this family."

He laughed. "She's already been on the phone with Grandma and Mrs. Bettencourt," he added.

"Great."

"Ha! At least they don't call him "fisheyes" like mom called Carl Royer for the two months he dated Marta." Jason strolled over and gave her a hug.

"Sorry about the whatsherface thing," Charity said in an undertone and Jason laughed. "I can't get your back tonight on this."

Her big brother snorted and shrugged. "We'll have lunch soon and catch up. School is on break until after New Year's." Jason was a fifth grade teacher in nearby Sacramento.

"Hi, Daddy." She gave her dad a hug and he kissed her cheek.

"Evenin', sweetie. You look awful pretty. Your mother says I'm not supposed to tell you that if Gabriel Bettencourt gets fresh I'll squash him like a bug. So I won't."

She rolled her eyes even though, at over six-and-a-half feet, her father's threat wasn't an idle one. He was a big man albeit one of the gentlest she'd ever known.

"All right then, I didn't hear it." She winked at him. "I just stopped in to say hello. I need to get going." But before Charity could make her exit, her grandmother on her dad's side came into the room. She didn't see them as often as her maternal grandparents as they lived part of the year in Palm Springs. "Gran!" Charity moved to hug her and accept a red lipsticked smack on the forehead.

At Christmas they gathered in Davis and at Easter they went to Pomona where her dad's brother and his family lived. Her maternal grandparents had the biggest house of the family in Davis so the Harrises and the Silvas all gathered there and spent the entire day eating, opening presents, napping and eating some more. They'd all start to gather in town over the next few days.

Smiling as she looked through her parents' living room and seeing those she loved sprawling in every open space, Charity knew how lucky she was. Still, she was bordering on late and she had some sprucing up to do before Gabe arrived.

"I have to go. I have a guest coming for dinner. I'll see everyone for brunch tomorrow," she called out, heading toward the door.

"Wait! Here, I made a few things." Her mother yanked her into the kitchen and Charity burst out laughing when she saw the bags of food on the table.

"Mom! A *few* things?"

"What? I had an extra roast. It'll just go to waste here. I also had some extra pies. Pecan, I recall Gabriel likes those. And a dutch apple. Some bread. Odd and ends really."

"Who has an extra roast? An *entire* roast?"

"I do. You want to argue with the woman who gave you

life?" Her mother drew her mouth into a mock frown and Charity thanked her as she dutifully took the bags.

Marta helped her get it all to her car. "You better tell me every detail."

"You'll just tell Ruben." Ruben was Marta's fiancé. They were due to get married in March. Her parents thought the sun rose and set in Ruben's ass. He was a nice guy and all and he treated Marta like a queen so as long as he did, Charity liked him too. He was also part of the little crew Gabe, Rafe and the other guys in their circle ran with.

"Ruben probably knows. He's due over here in an hour anyway. I have to tell him to reward him for spending the evening here."

"I'll talk to you later and yes, I'll give you details."

Gabriel paced in his front hall. Since he'd taken over operations at the dairy, he'd taken over the ranch style house his parents used to live in when his grandparents ran the dairy. Sighing, he headed back into his bedroom and changed his shirt yet again. This time back into the simpler button-down shirt instead of the dress shirt he'd put on earlier.

He'd psyched himself out. This wasn't a big date. He'd been friends with Charity forever, long enough she was like one of his family. He'd go over there and they'd have dinner, he'd explain that he wasn't the man for her and they'd enjoy a meal. He'd come home, masturbate like a fiend and fall asleep wanting her like he had for over a decade.

This was just dinner with a friend. Period. End of story.

So why did he show up on her front steps holding a bouquet of flowers, a bottle of wine and some chocolates?

It's only a wonder of nature why he didn't drop it all when she opened her door wearing an outfit that set all his hot for teacher fantasies aflame. Her hair sat on the top of her head in a loose bun, curls had escaped and she wore her glasses instead of her contacts.

The dress she wore was buttoned up high, even had a bow at the neck. It wasn't obscene. It wasn't showy in any sense but there was something about what it *didn't* show that made him crazy.

Her long legs peeked from the skirt, which hit her at mid thigh and she had on those shoes he loved, high heels, round toes and the strap over the front of her foot. And good Lord, did she have hose on?

"Hi there, oh are those for me?" She smiled and he forgot all his reasons for distance. Instead he leaned in and brushed his lips over hers.

That's when he caught her scent. Oh man, he was such a sucker for women who chose no perfume at all or more natural, earthy scents. This was, mmmm, he didn't know but he liked it.

"I like the way you smell," he heard himself saying and she blushed.

"Thank you. It's essential oil. Marta makes it. Frangipani. Come in."

The skirt swayed around her legs as she moved back to let him in and he felt like he was seventeen again.

"I hope you're hungry. I'd planned on something simple and light. Shrimp and some rice, a salad. However, you're getting pot roast, roast red potatoes, *coives* and the potato salad I know you like."

"Wow. Why the change in program? Not that I'm complaining."

"Come through to the dining room. Have a seat while I open the wine." She motioned to the small table heaped with food. "You'll probably know by tomorrow anyway but my mother wanted me to come to dinner there tonight. You know how my family comes into town and all for Christmas. Anyway, when I

169

said no I had to say why and that I was making you dinner. Apparently she thinks little of my cooking skills."

"Your mom has mad skills in the kitchen so it's all good with me. But I'm sure I would have loved the shrimp too." All he really wanted to eat stood before him. Damn it, ever since that kiss the night before, he'd lost rein on the need he'd had for her.

"Good answer. There's ice cream and pie too. Pecan. It's in the oven keeping warm so the ice cream will be all melty."

How was he going to resist her?

"Here." She began to make him a plate, putting several large slices of pot roast on it. "Potatoes? Or would you rather do it yourself?"

Not that he'd ever say it out loud but he loved being served by a woman. Not just any woman. Not a weak woman or a passive woman. No, he loved it when a strong willed woman took care of him, when she put that aside and did things for him. What? Some men had rubber fetishes, he liked it when a woman went all Donna Reed.

"N-no, that's fine. Some of everything, please."

She smiled. "Great. In that basket to your left are some rolls. Sweet and sourdough too. The butter is yours. I mean, from the dairy."

Damn, her mother was a good cook. Everything was delicious and perfectly seasoned. Admittedly, he was spoiled because he ate with his parents a few times a week and his mother routinely brought leftovers to him so even when he ate at home, it was good stuff. He wasn't a loser in the kitchen or anything, he could cook too. But he wasn't in this league at all.

"This is really good. Thanks for inviting me. Or let's be honest, thanks for ordering me over." He grinned and she laughed.

"Years of trying to be subtle got me group dates with pizza, eight people and crappy beer. I figured it was time to make a point."

She might have that Donna Reed thing going with the making of his plate but Charity Harris was a bulldog. Which, insanely, only made him want her more. The women he chose most often were showy on the outside but he set the pace, he began it and he ended it. What made Charity so dangerous was that she was precisely the kind of woman he craved. He'd be lying if he denied that her being Portuguese didn't appeal. She shared his heritage, shared the way he grew up and carried it into the next generation. She was ambitious, smart, soft in the best ways and hard where she needed to be. A woman like Charity Harris was wife material in the best possible way.

If he thought he could turn off his sexual desires, he'd have pursued her years ago. But he'd tried that route. Tried to be satisfied with sex where he pushed the darkness back. And he hated himself and the woman he was with because of it.

He admired Charity and the last thing he wanted was to end up resenting her and himself over it.

"Are you happy you came back to Davis instead of taking that job in LA at the TV station?"

She sat back in her chair and sipped her wine. "Really? Gabriel, are we going to do it this way? Fine, I'll play. For now. I came back because family is important to me. I wanted to be here and not hours away. I interned at the station, it was a good offer for an entrance level job but when I came back to town and saw the open storefront where Second Time Around is now, I saw myself there. I love to find treasures for people, I love what I do. I was raised with this idea of community values and spirit and it seemed like a good way to give back and to build a life for myself."

He watched as she buttered the roll and ate it, closing her eyes briefly as she did, clearly enjoying it.

"I liked LA. I still have friends there and I go to the Rose

Bowl Flea Market at least once every two months so I meet up with them. But in the end, I couldn't see myself there the way I am here."

Why did she have to say all that?

"Wasn't there anyone special there?"

"I was in a serious relationship in college, yes. Two actually. But they didn't feel the same way about family I did. They were both really nice guys, don't get me wrong. But neither could understand that I *like* being with family. They're not an obligation I hold my breath and deal with. I could never be with someone who didn't have those values. Men like, well, like Kevin and Brian, Belle's brothers, or Rafe. You even if you stopped being such a tool."

He laughed. "I'm a tool?"

"Why are you avoiding the subject? We both know why you're here." She stood and began to clear away the dinner dishes. He helped her, startled by their easy rhythm in the kitchen.

He could tell she was upset, her mouth, that luscious, gorgeous mouth of hers, compressed into a hard line.

Wanting to soothe her, he turned her to face him. "Honey, don't be upset. I just think we're better as friends. It's not about you."

"Oh my God!" She slammed her hand down and apple pie flew everywhere. She looked down and saw she'd put her fist into the pie dish. "Look what you made me do with that *it's not you it's me* bullshit!"

Fascinated, he watched her eyes flash, her face flush and, he couldn't miss that her nipples pressed against the front of that dress. He groaned.

Her angry movements were precise and mechanical as she wiped her hands off on a kitchen towel before she finally turned her attention back to him. "For the record, of course it's you. I

172

am *normal.* I can admit when I want something. I can talk about things instead of pretending they don't exist. What is your problem? You tell me right now and I'll back off. Give me a real reason why you treat me like I have cooties when you're staring at my nipples like you want to lick them."

He dragged his gaze back up to her face. A bit of the crumble topping from the pie had landed on her cheek and even though he knew he shouldn't, he reached up to flick it away but ended up kissing it instead. The sweetness of the sugar melted on his lips as her taste married with it.

Chapter Five

Just one taste...

She froze, not tense, but waiting. He took her mouth and she sighed into the kiss, molding her body to his and he felt every lush curve.

And that one taste exploded within him and there was nothing but his need for her, nothing but her scent in his nose, her taste on his lips, her moans in his ears, her ass in his hands as he pulled her closer.

She sucked his tongue and it shot straight to his cock. Trying to swim to the surface of his desire, he pulled away, trying to breathe air she wasn't heavy in, but she grabbed the front of his shirt and hauled him back.

"Oh no you don't, Gabriel. Give me more, damn you."

With a groan, he was lost, his mouth finding the fine line of her neck just above the collar of her dress. Without even thinking, her breasts filled his hands and she arched, whispering a tortured *yes*.

Okay so just this. He'd touch her. Through the dress. Kiss her some more and then he'd stop.

Charity felt his resolve melting as triumph filled her. *This* was what they should have shared before. There was something barely leashed about him and she wanted more. The edge of it titillated her, sent shivers through her body.

She heard the sound of the pins holding her hair hit the floor and counter as it fell around her face. One handed, he pulled her head back, exposing her neck while the other hand untied the bow at the neck of the dress and began to unbutton it. Oh yes oh yes! Her entire body threw a party and sang hallelujah as he skated his mouth, hot and wet, across her neck and down, over the curve of her cleavage.

She was wet, so wet and so turned on she squeezed her thighs together and ripples of pleasure echoed through her. His fingers tightened in her hair as he brought his mouth up to kiss her again. She'd never been handled before, not like this. Rough but not violent, so very in charge. The earth beneath her feet was insubstantial as her buttons were pushed in a way she'd never even imagined.

Horizontal. They needed two things—to be naked and horizontal. She backed toward her stairs, bringing him with her. He paused and she might have let out an actual growl.

"If you stop, I'll tell everyone in town you wear women's underpants. Don't test me."

He looked into her face, his eyes clearing a bit and then laughed. "Don't walk backwards in those heels, you'll fall." And with that, he picked her up, tossing her over his shoulder like a sack of feed and took them upstairs and into her room.

Before he could back out, she finished unbuttoning her dress and let it fall into a pool of fabric at her feet.

He exhaled, blinking as he took her in, garter belt, stockings, no panties and a push up bra designed to highlight her natural attributes. "Beautiful. So fucking beautiful I don't know where to look first."

"Show me, Gabriel. I want to see you."

"Come over here then and undress me."

She blinked and moved quickly, bending to grab the dress

and toss it in a nearby chair before working on his shirt.

Eight years ago, he was just barely out of his teens. The chest before her was all man. Work hard, strong, broad and hot to the touch of her lips as she kissed the spot over his heart. She pushed the shirt from his torso and placed it with her dress before moving back to his pants.

"Sit on the bed so I can get your boots off."

"If I sit on your bed there's no turning back," he said like a warning, his voice so taut she thought it might break.

She straightened and took her bra off. "Does it look to you like I want to turn back?"

"Christ." He sat, his gaze latched on her nipples. She let her hair slide to cover her face and hide her satisfied smile.

She liked taking care of him this way. Liked taking his boots off, then his jeans and socks. He stood once more and she knelt still, ending up looking straight at the very real evidence that he didn't want to turn back either.

Gabe looked down at her and got weak at the beauty of this woman on her knees before him. She couldn't possibly know how many times he'd jerked off imagining this very moment.

She reached up and pulled his boxers down and he stepped out of them, bending and hauling her up to the bed, laying her down and rolling on top of her body.

He wanted to mark her, wanted to grip her wrists while he thrust deep, wanted to take that spot on the side of her luscious breast between his teeth. She challenged his control. He owed her roses and sweet words but he wanted to hear her moan as he took her to that edge of pleasure/pain.

"Don't you dare," she said, her eyes searching his face, seeing his internal battle. "Don't hold back. I want all of you." She rolled her hips and the hot, wet embrace of her pussy against his cock nearly did him in.

"I'm not..." He choked back the words, shaking his head. He'd allow himself this taste of her and worry about the repercussions later.

Instead of saying anything else, he took her hair and wrapped it around his fist, angling her mouth just how he needed it and kissed her. *Really* kissed her. He gave in and let himself possess her the way he'd wanted to for so very long.

Shivers ran through him where her hands caressed over the planes of his back, he groaned into her mouth when her nails dug into his ass as she tried to get him closer.

"Mmm, you taste good." He dragged his tongue across her lips but pulled his groin away from hers, liking the desperate little sound she made in response. "Ah, ah, ah. I decide when you get more."

He waited for her anger but instead her eyes widened and her breath caught as she stilled. Smiling, he moved down a bit so he could finally give her nipples the attention he hadn't all those years before.

Kneeling, straddling her body, he took each mound into his palm and drew his hand away, taking her nipples between his fingers, pinching and rolling until she arched into his touch with a moan. Her hands sought his cock but he wanted this to be about her for the time being.

"Hands above your head. Clasp them."

Swallowing as she kept her gaze on him, she obeyed and he doubted he'd seen a more appealing sight than her breasts offered up to him with her back arched.

"Beautiful," he murmured as he bent, licking over first one nipple and then the other. She writhed beneath him and when he dragged his teeth across the sensitive tip she sucked in air. He waited to see if it was a pain response but she pressed herself against him again. It would be a matter of watching her responses, he wanted to do everything he'd ever imagined doing to her, things he hadn't done with anyone, but God knew he had to keep control and not send her weeping into the night.

Her skin was velvet soft, warm to the touch, richly fragrant with arousal and her essential oil. The muscles in her belly jumped as he kissed lower. He was glad she'd left the stockings and garters on. The absence of panties had been a surprise, a happy one of course. He just hadn't expected her to be a no panties kind of woman.

Her mound was smooth as he trailed the tip of his tongue over it. She spread her thighs to admit him as he traced the top of her thigh where the stocking met the hook of the garter belt.

"This is very sexy. I like it."

She lifted her head to look at him. It pleased him beyond words that she hadn't moved her hands from above her head. Her face was flushed, her hair mussed, lips swollen.

"I hoped you'd find out I was wearing them."

He spread her open and took a lick. Her taste shot through him, echoing off his insides. Damn, she tasted good. Right.

This was *so* much better than eight years ago. Charity let her head fall back. She gripped her hands together tighter to keep from reaching out to touch him. This rough-edged thing was seriously hot, and holy moley did he know how to go down on a woman. He'd clearly stepped up his game over the years.

His fingers dug into the soft flesh of her upper thighs as he just pushed his face against her and delivered the best apology for prior bad sex a girl could ask for.

Until he pulled away, actually making her whimper.

"Turn around. I want your ass in the air and your head down."

It took her a second to move, she was so enthralled by the command. *A command.* Imagine that. And imagine even more that she actually did it! When he danced his fingertips down her spine, shivers broke out. Until he cracked his palm against her left ass cheek, making her gasp. She let her eyes slide closed as she simply let herself experience the way it felt as he blew over the heat left behind.

He spread her open from behind and she squirmed, feeling totally exposed. His palm hit the other cheek and again the blowing. She began to have a whole new opinion of spanking as her nipples hardened where they brushed against the blankets below her.

When he went back to her pussy she cringed inwardly.

"Why are you pulling away?" he asked before sucking on her clit a moment, sending a wave of staggering pleasure through her.

"Huh?" What did he ask? Why wasn't he doing that more?

"When I eat your pussy from behind, you keep wincing. Am I hurting you?"

Oh that.

"It just...I feel very exposed that way."

"Good. Don't you know how beautiful you are from this vantage? Your garters sliding down the center of your thighs, framing your beautiful cunt? Your ass is fucking perfect, Charity. Round and full."

He drew his fingertip over the hidden star of her ass and she squealed in surprise.

He laughed. "I take it you don't get much action back here?" He slid two fingers into her pussy and then back up against her rear passage, pressing just enough to send all sorts of unexpected sensations through her.

"No," she answered honestly, albeit sort of breathlessly. And hello, she was exposed from stem to stern back there! Jeez, what woman wanted that sort of scrutiny?

"I like you this way." He said it and meant it. There was

more than a simple statement in the words and while she was admittedly flattered, she realized he liked things to be the way he wanted them.

And that was all right too. She'd known him a long time. She wouldn't have done this for anyone else. But for him, well for Gabriel Bettencourt, Charity couldn't imagine too much she wouldn't try at least once.

She let the tension fall away and he petted his hands over the curve of her ass. "Mmm, that's the way. Trust me, Charity. I won't hurt you, although I can't say I don't bring a little pleasure edged with pain."

Oh. Gabriel Bettencourt was already sexy, but this stuff? This hidden, dark stuff really blew her skirt up. She wanted to please him, wanted to show him she accepted that and more than just accepting it, she liked it.

She gasped a deep breath in and out when his mouth found her pussy again and she nearly wept at how good it felt.

Gabriel wanted to live in the moment when she came for hours and hours. It was a sort of accounting he needed to pay for the way he acted before but also, the sweetness of how she'd let go into him was intoxicating.

Her soft gasps and murmurs were almost as beautiful as the way she tasted and the softness of her thighs against his palms.

When he drew back, licking his lips, he saw his palm print marking the skin of her left ass cheek. He had to draw in a steadying breath, the sight of it staggered him. He could *not* have her. He couldn't have this with her. He needed to remember that. This would be one night and then it would be over.

That confidence in his decision slipped a bit when he noted she still clasped her hands together above her head, even after she'd rolled over. Had she forgotten or was she simply that obedient?

"Be back in a sec. Don't move."

She stayed motionless as he eased off the bed to get a condom from his pants.

What the hell was he doing? She was beautiful and soft, she'd been with him during some rough times. Had visited the hospital when his father was recovering from a stroke. She'd pitched in when they'd had damage from a windstorm and had to clean up the mess. Yes she could damned well be the wife of a man like him who worked with his hands. But at the same time he wasn't what she needed and there he was getting ready to stick his cock in her. He would ruin it. She was a good thing in his life. Bright. Kind and full of all the things he would hate to live without.

"Gabriel, if you leave me right now, if you walk out of here right now I'll never speak to you again. I was joking earlier, but now I'm serious."

Even as she spoke, she stayed in place and he lost his fucking mind. In moments he had the condom on and was kneeling behind her, guiding himself into her body.

Jaw clenched, body tense at holding himself back from slamming into her, he took his time as her body surrounded his.

"I can't be still," she whispered, catching his attention.

"You can't?" He edged into her a bit more. "Why is that?"

"I need more. Please."

He closed his eyes, done for. But still, she didn't move. So he gave her more, sliding all the way home, bringing the sweetest gasp from her.

"What is it you need, baby? Tell me and I just might give it to you." He kept his pace slow, knowing she wanted it hard and fast. Torturing himself as well as her.

"Harder and deeper and let me move. I want to push back against you," she said breathlessly, her fingers clutching the blankets where she still clasped her hands.

He delivered four deep, hard thrusts, his head cocked to the side so he could watch the rather delightful bounce of her breasts as he did it.

"Like that?"

She hissed her answer.

"You can move back against me. Keep your hands where they are."

Released from his order to keep still, she arched her back and pushed against him as he fucked into her. The curve of that fantastic ass fit perfectly in the cradle of his hips. She fit right, everywhere she touched him.

Screwing his eyes shut tight, he thought only of how good it felt to be buried so deep inside her. He would not think of anything else, damn it.

Over and over, he entered her deep and hard and retreated. She moved with him, keeping her cunt wrapped around him as much as she could and before long, he was this close to coming.

He reached around and found her clit, still slippery from when he'd used his mouth on her. Sliding it gently between his thumb and forefinger, he squeezed and brushed her clit with the pads of his fingers until she cried out and her cunt clamped around his cock so hard he was done for as she came around him.

Charity was still tingling, her muscles still jumping, when Gabriel returned to her bed. He drew a gentle line down her spine with his fingers. "You can move now."

She rolled to her back and looked up at him, tousled, sexy and so very pleased with a job well done.

"I must say, that was better than pie."

He laughed and reached for his pants.

"Where are you rushing off to so fast?" She arched a little, enjoying the way his hands missed the pants in the chair when he caught sight of her breasts.

"It's getting late."

She sat up, not bothering to cover her nakedness. "If this were any other night, you'd be here until way past midnight watching movies and eating me out of house and home." She blushed, remembering what he did eat.

Apparently he did too because his eyes darkened and he took three steps to the bed before he stopped himself. She narrowed her eyes at him.

"This isn't just any other night, though."

"No, it isn't. You finally admitted you wanted more than being friends." Which wasn't exactly what he'd admitted but so what? It was what he was going to admit by the time she was done with him.

He scrubbed his hands over his face and she wanted to laugh. He was *so* not going to win this. She wanted more, he did too even though he was holding back for some reason.

"Charity, this was...it was nice. But it can't happen again."

She burst out laughing. "Nice? You shut up, you big fat liar. Nice. Hah! It was hot. It was good. It was spectacular and you know it. Here I spent all this time wondering if I was horrible in bed and that's why you never came back. But I know now. We have amazing sexual chemistry. Not *nice,* not okay, but amazing. Why don't you just tell me what the deal is?"

"I don't want a relationship, Charity and you're a relationship sort of girl."

She scrambled to her feet. "Who says? Scared, Gabriel? Worried that you don't have what it takes to keep me satisfied?" she taunted when in truth, she was the scared one. Scared he'd walk away. Scared he meant it. But he couldn't. They had something more than just fun in bed, she knew it.

He clenched his jaw and his eyes went hot and dark and she knew she had him.

"You know it's not about that."

She inched closer, noting how his breath hitched. "Then tell me what it's about. I'm not looking to be married. We're already friends. We're good in bed. What's the issue? Do you like boys? Cows? What? Why are you hedging around what the real issue is? Are you embarrassed? Do you have, like, erectile dysfunction or are you incontinent?"

He tried to hold back a grin but lost the battle. "God you're a pain in the ass for a woman who's so pretty. No, I'm not incontinent, I don't want to fuck men or cows for that matter and did my cock feel like it had any dysfunction to you?" He pulled his jeans on but remained shirtless.

Charity pulled the shirt from his hands and put it on, loving that it still held his scent. That and she was not above manipulating him by wearing his shirt. She undid the garter belt and rolled the stockings down, forgoing any panties. His eyes never left her body as she moved.

"I need pie." He turned and walked out and she followed, slowly because the sight of Gabriel Bettencourt shirtless, ambling through her house looking sexed up and slightly miffed was something she wanted to commit to memory.

"Sit down," she said and he eased himself into a chair at the table she indicated. He watched her as she pulled the pecan pie from the oven and then the ice cream from the freezer.

Efficiently and gracefully, she reached into the cabinet, pulled down two mugs and poured coffee into them, placing them both on the table.

"Cream and sugar are right there." She pointed and turned

around to slice the pie.

He stirred slowly, mesmerized by the sight of her thighs peeking from beneath the hem of his shirt. She'd gotten rid of the garter and stockings before they'd come out of her bedroom but he liked this side of her too. Liked it a whole lot in his damned shirt.

"It's decaf." She slid a huge slice of pie with the promised melty vanilla ice cream on top before him and placed a fork and napkin beside it. "Was there enough cream in the container? I topped it up earlier."

Unable to help himself, he touched her hand, wrapping hers with his own. He kissed her palm. "Tastes a bit like apple pie." He grinned at her grimace. "There's plenty of cream here and enough pie and ice cream to feed four people."

She pulled her hand away and grabbed her own plate, with jumbled up apple pie and ice cream and sat next to him. He contemplated eating and leaving before she could ask him anything else but she turned those eyes on him and he knew he owed her the truth.

"Charity, you're a beautiful woman. Desirable. Funny and smart and your heart is big. We do have great sexual chemistry but we're friends and I don't want to ruin it." He put a finger over her lips to silence her rebuttal and took a bite of the heavenly pie.

"I'm not looking for a relationship and as you might have noticed, I have certain, um proclivities. I'm a hard man. You deserve a man who'll be gentle with you. I want..."

"What?" she asked quietly.

"I want to do things to you, with you, for you, on you...things, well let's just say I know I'm all wrong for you. Baby, you need a man who doesn't have dark edges."

She looked at him for some time without speaking, sipping her coffee, eating her pie. Finally she nodded as if she'd come to a decision.

"Don't you think I'm the one best to decide what I want or like to have done to me? I liked the way you were just now. Did my body say otherwise? You didn't hurt me, Gabriel. You were hard, yes, but you didn't go too far. I liked it and you can't convince me I didn't. Now that we've established neither of us is looking to get married, that we like each other, like having sex and I like that you're rough, there's no reason to continue with this silliness about not having sex anymore. We'll have it until we don't want to. Now, would you like another slice of pie?"

He stared at her. He needed to just leave, to make a clean break and they'd rebuild their friendship later. But his shirt, yeah, he couldn't very well leave without his shirt and all. Anyway, she was right, it would go on for a while and then she'd move away from him on her own once she saw he wasn't marriage material. Until then, why not enjoy her? She seemed to be on board with the tamest part of himself he'd shown her upstairs, although he wondered if he'd scare her once he brought out the toys.

Chapter Six

"You look distracted. Is everything okay?" Marta asked her the next day as they worked in their mother's kitchen.

Charity gave her sister a brief overview of the night before as they put all the food out on the big table.

"Oh my God that is so hot." Marta fanned her face and their mother turned a glance their way, narrowing her eyes.

Charity smiled innocently and poured some milk for her grandmother.

"Charity, that was the last of the milk. I forgot to say so when I was making the biscuits. Why don't you run over to the dairy to get some?"

Her mother was so not obvious at all.

"Why don't you just send her to the market? It's closer." Jason sat down. "Anyway, it's time to eat."

Her father looked at her mother, knowing something was up but not precisely what. Charity loved how he took her direction on that sort of thing.

"It'll take all of ten minutes. The bread is still warming in the oven and the milk from the dairy tastes better." Her mother said it like she didn't have a darned thing up her sleeve. She handed Charity a ten dollar bill. "While you're at it, you know maybe you should invite Gabriel to brunch. If he's around and all. I haven't seen him in a while now."

Jason looked to their mother and back to Charity and finally it dawned on him what was going on. He just laughed and shook his head. "Good luck to him."

Her father thought that was hilarious and she just rolled her eyes at them all as she left. "I'm taking your car, Jason. It'll be faster."

Charity didn't wait to hear his bellow of outrage as she jogged to his Mustang and took off toward the dairy. Even though it was a Sunday, the dairy was open, not like cows took a holiday or anything.

Mrs. Bettencourt gave her a big smile when she walked in.

"Good morning, Mrs. Bettencourt. My mom sent me here for milk. There's a full house for brunch and we're all out." Charity went to the cold case and grabbed several half gallons and brought them over to the counter.

"You just missed Gabriel. He had to go to the train station to pick up my sister's son and his wife. They're joining us for Christmas. He was in a very good mood this morning. I hear you two had dinner last night." Beatriz raised a brow at her and gave her her change.

"We did have dinner." Charity paused. "I like Gabriel a lot. I have for as long as I can remember."

Beatriz's smile widened and she nodded.

"Gabriel, get the door please, my hands are full," Gabriel's mother yelled from the other room as he was on his way to answer the door already.

"Like I'd make her walk in here to get the door when I'm two feet away," he mumbled as he turned the knob and swung the door back, only to nearly lose his breath at the sight of Charity standing on his porch looking like ten kinds of gorgeous.

"Cold out here. You gonna invite me in?"

He stood back and pushed the screen door open for her. "Sorry. We're just about to have dinner." She smelled like cold air and of wood fires and he had to take a step back to keep from pressing his face into her hair to take a better whiff.

"I know. Here," she pressed a warm bowl into his hands, "take it to your mom. I told her I'd bring scalloped potatoes." She sashayed past and delivered hugs and kisses to most of his family.

"You're letting the cold air in. Shut the door." Rafe smirked from the doorway into the dining room.

"And close your mouth or you'll gather flies," Belle said in an undertone from her chair nearby.

Charity looked so pretty. So feminine and soft in the white angora sweater and the wide legged trousers she wore with it. Effortlessly elegant even. Crap. He looked down at his plain black long-sleeved shirt and jeans and thought about going back to his house to change.

"Gabriel! I need you to get the ham out of the oven. Raphael, get the big platter from off the top of the china hutch," his mother called from the kitchen.

Gabe headed toward her but stopped to send a glare at his cousin John, who was flirting up a storm with Charity. His head was bent toward her and her eyes danced as she laughed at something he'd said.

"John, make yourself useful in the kitchen. Carry something," he snarled and John slowly turned to look at him and then back at Charity.

"I'm just fine. Anyway, Aunt Beatriz told *you* to help." He turned back to Charity and to her credit, she looked at Gabriel and smiled so prettily his annoyance faded and automatically, he smiled back.

Didn't mean he wasn't going to knock the crap out of John

later though. Punk.

"I need to go say hello to your mother," Charity joined him as he walked into the kitchen.

Immediately, the joyful cries and shrieks of female greeting sounded all around him and he smiled again. His mother's face lit when she caught sight of Charity. He knew he'd been set up but it didn't matter.

Belle came in and they all began to set the table, chattering in a mix of English and Portuguese. Gabriel brushed past Charity as he brought the ham to the table, putting it down where his mother pointed. Rafe followed with a platter of chicken.

John moved to the chair nearest Charity once dinner had been announced but Gabriel sat instead. *"She's mine"* was the look he sent and John laughed, moving to sit elsewhere.

"Would you like some chicken, Gabriel?" Charity asked, taking his plate and filling it with food from the bowls and platters nearest to where she sat.

"Yes, thank you."

She even buttered two slices of bread for him.

"Charity, I wanted to invite you to Christmas Eve services with us this year. My memory is shot so I thought I'd ask while I remembered," his father said. Not his mother, but his father. Who knew?

Charity blushed and sent his dad such a look, even the gruff Bettencourt patriarch ducked his chin a moment.

"Thank you, Mr. Bettencourt. I'd love to. My family will be there too, of course."

"I've been telling you for years now that we're Anthony and Beatriz. You're like a member of our family. How many times have you spent the night here with Rosemary?" His father grinned and the woman in question, Gabe's baby sister, came into the house with her kids and husband, Ben.

More female squealing as Rosemary caught sight of Charity and Belle and they all hugged. Rafe and Gabriel got up to help Ben get the kids' stuff into the house and situated.

His niece Lettie was perched in Charity's lap when he came back into the dining room. Tonia, the middle niece rested in her grandpop's lap, happily eating off his plate and the only boy, Kit, slept in his grandma's arms.

Rosemary, Belle and Charity sat, heads together, laughing and talking. His mother looked at them and then to Gabriel and chuckled. He knew he was in for it. He knew it but right then he didn't care. She was his friend. This scene had played out before. Charity had been at their dinner table dozens of times over the years either there with Rosemary or with Gabe's group of friends. That it *was* different wasn't something he planned to examine.

However, when they were done with dinner, he was taking her back to his house and fucking her. Twice. He had plans for her. Then he'd know if she was just trash talking or if she really was okay with what he liked.

Charity loved the Bettencourts. Had loved them for a great deal of her life and now that this whatever-it-was, was growing with Gabriel, it felt natural to be there. There was no nervousness. They knew her, she knew them. Even Lourdes, Beatriz's mother who only came to Davis every other Christmas, liked her and the woman was notorious for scaring people! She'd helped Charity and Rosemary get ready for events when they were younger and had told them stories of her girlhood in the Azores.

This thing with Gabriel had been in the making for twenty years and even if he wanted to pretend not to see it, it was there. The way he looked at her was certainly there. Like she was the most beautiful woman in the room. He even blushed when she'd done small things for him like getting him a cup of coffee or a slice of cake. Silly little things. Goodness knew their mother spoiled Raphael and Gabriel shamelessly so it wasn't like he was unaccustomed to women doing things for him. But that he reacted so strongly when *she* did it just made her shivery all the way down to her toes.

She helped clean the kitchen with the other women as they sipped wine and swapped gossip about the people they knew. She fit there as easily as she did in her own family.

Still, she was surprised when he came up behind her and encircled her waist with his arms and rested his chin on her shoulder. "You look beautiful tonight."

"Thank you. So do you. Or, handsome I suppose."

"Do you have the time to stop by my place for a bit?" he asked quietly.

"I do. I don't have anywhere to be first thing." Not that he'd asked her to sleep over but she thought she'd put it out there anyway.

He turned with her, taking her hand. "Good night, all. I'm going to steal Charity now."

"Are you going to have your wicked way with me?" she asked as he drove her car back to his place.

"I was considering it. You have any problems with that plan?" He grinned as he pulled her car to a stop.

"Depends on how well you do it." She grinned back.

"Stay right there." He got out and came to open her door. Normally she'd do it herself but with him, she found she liked that he wanted to do little things for her.

He pulled her to his body as she stood to get out and crushed her mouth with his own for a kiss. She melted against him, savoring his taste, loving how hot he was against her body while the air outside was so cold.

The kiss was easy, but deepened the longer he held her. She opened to it, to him, loving the way he felt. He'd kissed her, he'd sought her out, he'd been affectionate and even possessive at dinner.

He looked into her eyes for long, tense moments after he broke the kiss.

"You ready?"

She nodded.

"Trust me?"

"I've known you for nearly thirty years. You've never done anything untrustworthy in all that time. Yes, I trust you or I wouldn't be here right now." She wished she could say everything she felt about him but she knew it would spook him.

He took her hand and drew her toward the house and into the front door. He locked it and turned back to her. "You know which one my bedroom is. I want you undressed and on the bed. On all fours. I'll join you in a moment." He paused, looking her up and down and her entire body seemed to vibrate at the blatantly sexual perusal. "Take your hair down. I like it against your bare skin. You're so beautiful."

She smiled, feeling shy all the sudden.

In his bedroom, breathless at being surrounded by his scent, she undressed and let her hair loose from the barrette. She got on his bed as he'd instructed and waited. The air caressed her bare skin as anticipation zinged through her veins.

In the guestroom, where Gabriel kept his toys, he removed his shoes and socks and went to the chest at the end of the bed and unlocked it. The scent of leather wafted up at him as he reached down and grabbed the crop and a blindfold.

The crop had the perfect amount of give to it, bending easily but not too easily. Springing back into place with a nice whoosh of air. The sound, the creak of the leather made his cock twitch as he walked back to his room.

He rarely used the crop. It wasn't something you could break out on a first date and he didn't tend to keep woman around for longer than a month or two. But when he'd bought it two years before, it had been Charity he'd thought of. It was getting harder and harder to ignore how it all came back to her, over and over. She was what he'd wanted for his entire adult life.

His pulse sped as he caught sight of her on his bed. *Mine.*

He put the crop down on the edge of the bed, where she could see it. He wanted to give her a chance to back out. Hope she would warred with hope she wouldn't. She froze and sucked in a breath.

"You okay?" He petted down the curve of her ass and his cock throbbed.

"Uh. Yes. I've never…"

"We can forgo it." He moved to pick it up but she shook her head.

"No. I want to. I want you to use it on me." Her voice was breathless but sure. She got to him, damn it. Truth was, she always had.

"Sure?"

"Show me, Gabriel. I've never done anything like this before. Show me more."

"You can *feel*. I'm going to cover your eyes."

"Okay," she breathed out in a barely audible whisper. Not a scared whisper.

He groaned and slid the blindfold over her eyes, making sure it was light tight and comfortable. Her skin immediately broke out in gooseflesh and she breathed out slowly.

"You look so fucking beautiful here on your hands and

knees." She did. It made every cell within him yearn to have this all the time. Instead he picked the crop up and drew a line down her spine with the tip. Around to her breasts and those nipples that made his mouth water and his hands itch to touch. "The curve of your breasts, your nipples so dark and hard—so gorgeous. And your ass, oh that pretty ass of yours." He smoothed his palms over the solid, rounded muscle of her cheeks, giving each one a crack of his opened hand.

She wriggled back against him and he smiled. Maybe they could enjoy each other more than he first thought.

He traced the tip of the crop over the seam of her ass. He wasn't a stranger to crops, having grown up in rural America and all. But it was a skill that needed practice and honing.

A quick switch of his wrist and he landed a sharp snap against her thighs, just below the curve of her ass.

"Oh!" She squirmed and he couldn't tear his eyes from the red line he'd made on her flesh.

Oh indeed.

Again and again, he landed the crop against her butt and her thighs. More for the sound than the actual strike, although he did love the webwork of red lines from the crop. He watched her carefully, noting her reactions, making sure to keep her on the right side of the pleasure/pain divide. Creating a heat but not a burn. He loved the careful creation of the experience for her, wanted her first time to be something she'd always remember after she'd married a guy like Brian and thought back to the wild fling she'd had with that very bad boy back in the day.

Her head drooped and her breathing deepened as she slowly became drunk with the sum of everything he did. Could it be possible that she'd gone into subspace? Surely not her first time out?

He tossed the crop aside and blew over the heated,

reddened skin. She moaned, low and deep. Her thighs glistened, she was so wet. He traced a fingertip over engorged, juicy labia and she thrust her ass back to him.

Anything else he could have handled. But this? The way she'd submitted and liked it, really liked it given the state of her thighs, had broken him down. He needed her with an intensity he didn't quite know how to process.

Making sure she was all right and still on board with the program, he quickly got rid of his shirt and pants and positioned himself behind her. Rolling a condom on his cock nearly sent him over the damned edge he was so turned on.

Fighting against the urge to slam into her, instead he took his time, pressing and retreating, getting a bit deeper each time until he was buried to the root.

Her skin was still hot from where he'd used the crop, the feel of it against his thighs created a delicious contrast. The inner walls of her body clutched at him even as she fit him like she was made just for his cock.

Charity swam through the depth of pleasure she was swamped in, surfacing to feel every bit of him as he thrust into her slowly, his fingertips tracing over the knobs of her spine.

He was so unexpected on every level. He'd just used a riding crop on her! And yet, he'd given her such an intensity of pleasure and sensation she'd never have been able to imagine. *This* was BDSM? She'd always thought of it like dudes in leather pants using face masks and chaining up their women in the corner and stuff. Come to think of it, Gabriel in leather pants would work and the idea of him tying her up wasn't one she was opposed to at all. Masks? Not so much. Or those gags with the rubber balls. So not for her.

But he seemed to be able to anticipate just what she'd like and he gave it to her. The blindfold thing really worked too. With her eyes still covered, she felt with more intensity. His touch, the way he fucked her, so gentle after the crop. Such sweetness after such raw sexual energy made her want to cry.

"So beautiful, you're so beautiful, baby," he whispered and she heard desire threading his voice.

He made her feel it, feel beautiful and adored. She didn't need to see his face just then to know how he looked at her. No one had ever looked at her that way. Why he seemed to fear it, when he was so good at it, when he seemed to *feel* it too made her sort of pissed off.

Tears pricked the back of her eyes. She wanted him to love her, to be okay with being with her. How would she get past his reserve?

On he went until she fell under the sway of whatever personal magic they made, just the two of them. His slow digs into her pussy built her up inexorably, filling her cells bit by bit with so much pleasure she wanted to explode from it even as she never wanted it to end.

"I'm coming...you too," he urged. "Make yourself come."

She braced her head down and levered one hand up to her clit, catching it between her middle and forefinger. Three slippery squeezes and she rocketed into climax with a gasped cry of his name and he shoved into her so deep she felt him tap her cervix as he followed.

"Be right back," he said, removing her blindfold and kissing her shoulder.

She collapsed on her belly, the cool sheets beneath her soothing as she caught her breath.

"Are you okay?" he asked, sliding into bed next to her. "I didn't hurt you?"

She turned her head to face him, smiling at his concern. "I'm more than okay. I feel lovely. You didn't hurt me. I had no idea at all. If someone had told me yesterday that being whipped with a crop could make me feel like that I wouldn't have believed them. I liked it, a lot. The blindfold gave me so much more sensation."

He returned her smile, lying on his side and she took a risk, snuggling into him and happily, he took her into his arms, kissing the top of her head.

"When can we do it again?"

Chapter Seven

Charity helped her mother do dishes and tried not to overanalyze the night before. Which was impossible.

She'd stayed until about 3 am and then had left. Charity had decent manners, she'd waited for him to ask her to stay but he hadn't and in the end, she'd gotten up and dressed. Instead he'd walked her to her car and watched her drive away.

It wasn't the first time she'd worked at the shop with less than four hours' sleep but her frustration had kept her awake until they'd closed up at one. Brunch at her house was more like a late lunch. Why they'd never started calling it lunch she didn't know but Sunday brunches were eaten at two pm. Period.

She hadn't bothered to ask Gabriel to join them, he'd pissed her off so much. More than that, it hurt a bit that she *knew* he felt something for her but ran from it so hard. Charity needed some space from him to lick her wounds and re-fortify herself for another round.

"So what's the deal between you and Gabriel?" Jason asked, taking the plate from her and drying it.

"According to him? Or according to me?"

Jason handed the towel to Jeremy and took her hand. "Let's go for a walk. Jer, take over."

Once they'd gotten a bit away from the house, the quiet of

the day hit her, calming her slightly.

"I've known Gabriel as long as you have. I've seen him with a lot of women. A lot of them. They come and they go without much of an impression in his life." Jason looked out over the horizon.

She took a deep breath. "Are you telling me it's hopeless? That he'll never settle down?"

"Is that what you want? To settle down?"

"I've spent pretty much every waking moment of the last week or so thinking about my feelings for Gabriel. And before that, I thought about it every few days and tried not to. Gabriel has been in my thoughts in some way or another pretty much since I was sixteen years old. You know what I realized last night?"

Her brother leaned against one of the almond trees in their yard and waited for her to speak.

"I'm in love with him. Yes I want to settle down. With Gabriel Bettencourt. So if you think it's hopeless tell me. If I keep this up and he pushes me away it's going to really hurt."

He reached out to squeeze her hand. "I don't think it's hopeless. You're already close to him. It's clear to anyone with eyes you two have major chemistry. I took a grain delivery out to the dairy today for dad. Gabriel, Rafe and I had coffee. You know what he talked about the whole time?"

"Me?" She knew she had all sorts of wistful hope in her voice but she couldn't help it.

"You're something else, you know that? And yeah, you. He tried not to. Told me he was all wrong for you. But when Gabe is done with a woman, he's done. There's no pillow talk, there's no sharing of funny anecdotes with his friends. Today he talked about how you were at dinner with his family. He talked about stuff we all did growing up. I want to tell you I don't think you should give up. He'd be a fool not to love you. But I need to know and you need to really ask yourself, *is* he the wrong guy for you? If yes, then let him go. Being unhappy isn't worth it. If he's the right guy, then fight for him and convince him he's precisely the *right* guy for you."

"You'd die from TMI if I told you what the issue is and I'm pretty sure I would too. But he's being so dumb about this *not right for you* thing."

Her brother looked uncomfortable for a moment and then sighed. "Is this a sex thing? Like he's into something super weird like diapers or something?"

She held back a laugh, not only at how her brother looked at the moment but at the thought of Gabriel thinking anyone believed he was into diapers.

"Well, gosh, you know, they make them in adult sizes now and since you knew, I guess it's not that big a secret."

He looked at her, his eyes widening in horror until she burst out laughing and then he socked her in the arm.

"I'm sorry, I had to! It is a sex thing yes, but it's not particularly weird and certainly not in the realm of diapers. I worry about your exposure to public schools, Jason, if this is what you're thinking about all day. Does Gina like this sort of stuff?"

"You suck. I'll get you for that. And for your information, Gina and I broke up."

"Oh no! Because of the whatsherface thing?"

"No. Mom was right. But don't tell her that. She and I just weren't right for each other although the sex, the non-diaper sex, was great, there was nothing else. I want to settle down too. I'm knocking on thirty years old in just a few months, I want a family of my own. She wasn't ready." He shrugged.

They walked back into the house, laughing, and she felt a lot better.

He'd wanted her to stay until he had to get up to work but hadn't asked. He knew he'd hurt her but he was desperate to keep distance between them. Especially after the way she'd been with him, so beautifully open and accepting, so sexual and exciting...he lay there in his bed and found himself falling for her in a way he'd never expected. The power of that scared the hell out of him.

She hadn't called or shown up that whole day. He knew her shop was open until one on Sundays so she could have come by any time after that. Of course, he could call her or drop by. They were friends. He'd done it before.

He made up his mind and headed to his truck, only to stop at his parents' house when he caught sight of her car out front.

"Hey, fancy seeing you here," Charity said calmly as he entered his mother's kitchen. Her hair was pulled back into a ponytail and she had on an apron. She stood at the table with his mom and sister, kneading bread and laughing.

"I think that's my line." It came out sharper than he'd intended and she physically reacted, her eyes meeting his and he didn't fail to catch the flash of hurt there.

Slowly, she stepped back and wiped her hands.

"I'm going to get going now. Just let my mom know when you're done with the trays and Jason will come by to get them."

His mother looked at him but couldn't make him feel any worse than he already did.

"Charity, wait. I didn't mean it the way it came out," he said, following her as she tossed the apron on a chair and headed outside with her coat and purse clutched against her body like a shield.

She moved pretty fast but he had her blocked in.

He caught up to her at her car. "Wait, damn it. I'm sorry."

"I want to go."

He heard the tears in her voice and gently, he tipped her chin up so he could see into her face. A face so familiar to him he wouldn't know what to do if it wasn't part of his life.

"I didn't mean for that to come out that way. I was on my way to your house when I saw your car here. I'm sorry." Not able to do anything else, he brushed his mouth over the curve of her bottom lip. "Don't look that way, baby. I didn't mean to make you sad. Will you let me take you to dinner? To make up for it?"

She nodded and he pulled her close, happy when she hugged him back.

At the little Thai place near the campus, she sat across from him at a rickety table and he was suddenly aware of just how many people stared at her. She didn't have a lot of makeup on and she wore a pair of jeans and a black sweater but still, something about her drew a man's eye.

"You were really on your way to my house or did you just say that because you thought I might cry?" she asked, using chopsticks like a pro while he'd already given up and began using his fork.

"I really was on my way to your house. I hadn't seen you all day. I thought I'd see if you wanted to grab some dinner. I hadn't expected to see you kneading bread in my mom's kitchen. It just took me by surprise."

"A bad surprise?"

No, a good one. He'd *liked* how she looked there, her face lit with laughter as she'd worked next to his two favorite women in the world.

"No. Why would you say that? I was on my way to see you, why would seeing you be a bad thing?"

"Okay, okay. You're just so touchy! I didn't know. I don't want to eat anymore. I want to have sex." She turned those green eyes his way and he felt it straight to his toes.

He nearly choked to death on his pad thai as she calmly asked for, and received, boxes for their food and packed it away.

He managed to pay and not get into an accident on the way back to her place and thankfully, she stayed over on her side of the truck so he could halfway think.

"I liked seeing you in my mom's kitchen tonight, your hands in the bread, a bit of your hair had escaped the ponytail and you blew it out of your face. You even had a spot of flour on your cheek. All in all, pretty damned hot." It wasn't candlelight and romance but she deserved to know part of what she did to him.

He pulled into a parking spot and she scooted over, sliding into his lap to face him. "You know, I can be so mad at you one minute and then you make me all melty the next."

"I'm about to make you a lot more melty," he said in a low growl. "Let's go."

"Do you really want to? You know, you're not the only one who has a bit of kink in his laces." She leaned back a bit and ran her hands up her torso, over her breasts, giving in to a little sigh of satisfaction as she touched her nipples. All he heard was his struggle for breath and the white noise of what was most likely an impending stroke.

"Oh yeah? What else have you got then?" he asked her, watching her every move.

She pulled her sweater up and off, facing him, those luscious breasts barely covered by a lacy bra.

"Show me your breasts. Touch your nipples for me." Hell, his voice sounded hoarse even to his own ears.

He heard her swallow, but then she obeyed, leaning into him to reach around and unhook her bra, sliding it down her arms, her breasts jiggling a bit with the movement. She wet her fingers, her eyes locked on his, and played her thumb and forefinger against her nipples, churning her hips over his cock.

The scent of her body filled the cab of the truck.

"I wish you had a skirt on. I'd have you finger yourself right here in the open. But since you don't, pull your sweater back on so I can get you inside. Then we'll continue this."

She moved, slow and graceful, to get her sweater on. Once that was done, he simply grabbed her about the waist and hauled her from the truck with him and headed to her front door.

She stood, waiting for him to lead her and it nearly felled him.

"Get naked for me." He moved to sit on her couch, turning on the lamp and watching her expose every beautiful inch of her skin. When she was done, she released her hair from the ponytail and he shivered at the sight of it falling around her shoulders.

He leaned back. "Come here, sit on my lap."

She knew what he wanted, sat on him, spreading her thighs outside his, her breasts just inches from his mouth. He caressed up her thighs, into the curve of her waist, took the weight of her breasts, thumbing over her nipples until she made soft sounds at the back of her throat.

"I love the way your pussy smells. Almost as good as it tastes." He circled her clit with his middle finger and then traced over her lips before kissing her.

"Every time I even think of you, you make me wet," she whispered against his mouth as he moved from the kiss.

"Christ," he hissed. The mixture of her, of Charity, sweet but with this naughty side got to him, dug under his skin. "Touch your pussy. Make yourself come for me."

He couldn't look away from the descent of one hand down her belly. He sucked in air as she spread herself open enough to play against her clit with her middle finger.

Her breath caught at the bolt of pleasure.

"L-like this? Shall I stop?" His eyes on her, the way he looked at her like she was the best thing he'd ever clapped eyes on, fired some inner strength. She felt like a goddess up there on his lap. Sexy. Powerful.

"Yes, just like that. And don't stop unless you want to kill me. Make yourself come. And then we're going up to your bedroom." He laced his fingers behind his head and relaxed back against the pillows, just watching.

She tugged on her nipple and brushed the pad of her middle finger from side to side over her clit, her hips moving as orgasm stole toward her, blurring the edges of the world outside the space she and Gabriel inhabited.

His body was warm beneath her, the sound of his breath as he watched her echoed against her own. It wasn't like she'd never masturbated before, but in front of someone took a level of trust she never could quite work up. But she'd done it with him without even thinking. Even the week before after he'd brought her home from the bar.

Her head tipped back right as she began to come and the world exploded around her as he held her throat with one big hand. Not suffocatingly, not rough, but enough pressure to collar her that way. Never in her life had she felt anything like it. Trust that he wouldn't hurt her, excitement that he'd hold her that way. Her entire system lit up as she moaned.

Slowly, he relaxed his grip and shifted to put his arms around her, hugging her tight. She fell forward against him, breathing hard, wondering that he'd found yet another way to push all her buttons.

"You're so beautiful," he murmured against her hair. "I didn't scare you?"

She snuggled into him with a satisfied sigh. "No. It

was...unexpected. I've never felt anything like it. I...well obviously it worked for me."

He picked her up as if she weighed nothing, holding her against him as she wrapped her legs around his waist.

"Let's go see what else works for you," he said as he took them both upstairs and into her bedroom.

Chapter Eight

"Hey, um, would you be interested in helping me get a tree?"

Gabriel looked up to see Charity standing on his doorstep looking very festive in a red sweater and white jeans. His heart contracted at the way she looked and the way he'd missed her, and the sight of her made him happy. He'd never relied on a woman in that way before. Never counted on one to make him happy or fill him up the way she did.

She ducked her head a moment and looked up through her lashes. "I can ask someone else. I just thought since I was here already I'd stop and ask you. So then I can watch your muscles flex and stuff."

He laughed and kissed her. He'd simply accepted that he liked to touch her and did. His mother had invited her to dinner several times and he'd be going to a huge pre-Christmas brunch at her grandparents' house the following day.

She was suddenly just in his life. Not that she hadn't been before but he'd ached for her and pretended he didn't. He pretended she was just one of the gang. Now he didn't have to pretend. She was more than a friend, she was...a girlfriend? Um, no, not that. He wasn't right for her, nope. Now he had her in his bed, in her bed, wherever and whenever and she responded to him in ways he'd never imagined. That's what it was and he'd think about the rest after the holidays.

"Why do you wait so long to get a tree?" He opened the door wider to let her in. "Come in for a second so I can turn the computer off and get my boots on."

He sat in the chair nearest the door but before he could, she'd picked up his boots. She knelt and laced his boots quickly and efficiently. But it left him speechless. She did these things to him, *for* him and it touched some part deep inside. Things she didn't have to do, things he didn't need her to do but that she did them for him, took care of him left him off balance and unsettled. He didn't want to feel so deeply for her, damn it, he could not have her.

Instead, he drew his fingertips over her collarbone and she looked up, smiling. "Thank you."

She shrugged. "Anyway, I like waiting until two days before Christmas to get a tree. It's more fun that way. And it's not like I'm home on Christmas day at this point. So I have a tree for myself and enjoy the trimming." She blushed and took the hand he offered to help her up. "Would you like to stay for dinner after we get the tree? Help me trim it?"

"Yeah, I'd like that. We can order a pizza and watch those DVDs you rented." He grabbed his keys. "I'll meet you back at your house to drop your car off."

She laughed. "Um, no car. My mom came over. She brought my grandma to visit with your grandma. I rode over with them. I was hoping to throw myself on your mercy. You're very good at taking me in hand when I need it."

He took a steadying breath. "Be careful there, missy." He swatted her ass, only slightly playfully.

"I don't want to be careful, Gabriel," she said seriously as she got into the truck.

She stood back and watched him negotiate and load the tree into the back of his truck, all while she sipped the hot cider he'd insisted on buying her because he told her he hated to see her shiver.

The day before he'd shown up at the shop with warm sweet rolls and coffee. He'd insisted on fixing a loose board on her deck. He was a good man, good to her and those people he loved.

She hid her smile behind the cup, inhaling the fragrant steam and feeling very taken care of.

"Okay, all ready." He opened the door for her and she hopped into the truck.

Back at her place, he backed into the drive and waved her inside. "Get out of the cold, babe. I've got this. Just be ready to slide the stand with fresh water under the tree." Absently, as he began to untie the tree, he kissed the side of her mouth.

Gabriel sat, snuggled up on her couch, Charity tucked against his side. Christmas music played low on her stereo, the lights on the tree lit the room nicely along with the fire dancing in the fireplace.

"That was very good pizza. I hadn't tried that place yet. Nice call," she said lazily, her head on his shoulder.

"Glad you liked it. The tree looks good."

"You chose it, you hauled it and you set it up. I just put sparkly stuff on it. Oh!" She sat up and jogged from the room, returning within moments with two stockings. "Forgot these. Yours is bigger." She laughed suggestively and he snorted.

She got him a stocking for her mantle. It made him warm inside. "Thanks, what I want most won't fit in it. You're a C cup."

"Ha ha. Anyway, those are yours already. Don't mess up my simple pleasures, Gabriel. It's the little things."

He looked down at her socks, covered in reindeer with

shiny red noses and grinned. "Gotcha. Wouldn't dream of messing up any of your pleasures, Charity."

She moved to him sitting astride his lap and cupped his face in her hands. "Gabriel, thank you for today. For helping me." She kissed him and he let her lead instead of diving into her mouth like the heaven it was.

She tasted him in small kisses and flicks of her tongue. So soft and gentle but demanding too. He smiled against her mouth and she pulled back. "Do I amuse you?"

He laughed. "Yes. Come to midnight mass with us day after tomorrow," he blurted and she blinked, returning his smile.

"I'd be honored to go with you and your family, Gabriel. And will you have Christmas breakfast with my family?"

He knew it was big, as big as him asking her to go to mass with his family. These things were inviolate to both their families. Traditions that bound them all together. But he realized there wasn't any place he'd rather be than with her.

"Yeah, sounds good. Like I could say no to your mom and grandma's cooking. Of course then we'll have to head over to my family's for lunch."

She nodded, blinking fast to cover glossy, tear filled eyes. He'd done a big thing by asking her, by spending this special time with her and her family and inviting her into his. It meant something to her, that was plain on her face.

"Okay we're getting all mushy now and we're not supposed to. You've made me very hard and I think you need to take care of that."

She swallowed and began to slide off his lap but he changed his mind, bringing her back to kiss her, and rolling them both to the floor. She widened her thighs to take him, fitting herself to his body, anticipating what he'd want.

All he felt then was the rush of need in his ears as he peeled the clothes from her body, firelight on her olive skin, her eyes desire-lidded as she watched him above her. When he pushed his cock deep into her body she sighed, squirming a bit to accommodate him.

"Perfect," he whispered into her nipple as he licked around it before nipping it sharply.

Her nails dug into his sides where she held on as he thrust deeply. He couldn't wait, he had to have her right then with the memory of her sweet smile burned into his brain. He wanted to mark her even as he realized he wanted to rut on the floor with a woman who needed soft sheets.

But it wasn't enough. Knowing that wasn't enough to make him stop, especially when she moaned deep and low when he brought her knees to his sides, changing his angle.

Again he moved her legs, this time putting her feet on his shoulders, bending her as he continued to fuck her. He dominated her with his size, with his body. No other man had done this, no other would. Not ever. This would be theirs long after he'd gone.

Her cunt rippled around him as he ordered her to finger herself. It wasn't long before she began to come around him and he only lasted another two minutes after that before he joined her.

He pulled out carefully and made a quick trip to the bathroom to dispose of the condom. When he got back she'd pulled the couch pillows and a blanket down to the floor. On her belly, she sipped a beer, one long leg bent up, swinging back and forth lazily.

He winced when he saw the red on her ass.

"Gabriel David Bettencourt, you gave me rug burn," she said, turning around and looking stern for about thirty seconds. He'd been about to apologize until she laughed. "I've never had rug burn before. I do believe it was long past time."

The next day they arrived at her grandparents' house for brunch and were greeted by a nearly deafening chorus as they walked through the door.

He'd spent the night, knowing they had to be up early and his father had insisted on being in charge of operations at the dairy that particular day. It had been up to Gabriel most days as Rafe had his own work with Belle's family's farm and the other marketing he did for the dairy. He and Rafe traded off back and forth on occasion but each man had their share of four a.m. alarms going off. A few months back, Gabriel promoted his cousin to a foreman's position and now his four a.m. alarms were more like six and he even had days off.

His father liked to keep a hand in at the dairy though and his cousin would keep an eye on things, along with his mother, to make sure he didn't over do it.

He'd really liked waking up next to Charity. Her shop was closed until the day after Christmas so they'd slept in and had made love twice more after waking. A man could get used to opening his eyes and seeing Charity on the mattress next to him.

The house was overflowing with people from both sides of Charity's family but luckily he knew many of them. He caught sight of Ruben in a far corner talking with Jason.

Charity kissed the side of his neck. "Go on."

"Let me say hello to your parents first." He stifled a smile but kissed her quickly. "I like you."

She laughed as they headed into the kitchen where her mother manned a giant pot of something on the stove.

"Gabriel! It's wonderful to see you." Her mother wiped her hands on a towel and moved to accept a kiss and a hug.

Her grandmother Lourdes came over and he bent to take her hands and kiss both cheeks as he spoke to her quietly in Portuguese. She laughed with him, flirting and asking after his family.

Such a mixture in the house of redheads and fair skin from her dad's side and the darker hair and olive complexion from her mom's. Her father approached and gave him the once over.

"Mr. Harris, thanks for having me today."

"It's James, boy, and if you make Charity happy, that's all I need."

Gabriel nodded, feeling like a fake because he knew he wouldn't be there the following year.

"Game's on." James nodded and walked out.

"That was an invitation," Charity murmured and Gabriel kissed her cheek and followed, glad to see the den where the game was on filled with familiar faces.

Ruben nodded by way of greeting, shoved a soda into his hand and moved over a bit when he sat down.

Charity rushed home to shower and change before heading over to Gabriel's house for dinner. So busy her life was all the sudden!

Her jaw had nearly hit the floor when he invited her to midnight mass and then Christmas dinner. She knew he was beginning to accept the idea of them as a couple but that was huge. Mass and Christmas was their family's inner sanctum and he'd opened the doors up and invited her in. It meant something, told her he felt for her deeply and she dared to hope as deeply as she felt for him.

Her family already liked him. He'd hung out and watched football all afternoon. Her mother and both grandmothers had doted over him and he'd been a total sweetie pie with them, asking about their lives, flirting, helping them out with things needing to be moved or lifted without making them feel like they needed help.

He'd been charming and attentive and, as she stood in front of the mirror to check her hair, she was so far gone in love it wasn't funny. She'd looked for love over her adult life but hadn't felt any particular urgency about it. And it had been there all along, just readying itself.

At the same time, now that she'd admitted it, allowed herself to see it and feel it, raw, stark terror about whether or not Gabriel was ready to see it and feel it lived in her heart. She sensed a war within him and it scared her.

They were right for each other, she *knew* it. But if she couldn't show it to him, if he refused to see it, what difference would it make?

Gabriel sat in the pew and looked down to where he held Charity's hand. She sat next to him at Christmas Eve mass. He'd never had a woman beside him at mass he wasn't related to and he couldn't help but remember Belle coming with Rafe the year before.

After Christmas he had to make a break with her. He couldn't keep on any longer because he was used to her, attached to her. He missed it when she wasn't with him. He called her when she was at work. He wanted to wake up with her. None of that was part of the plan at all. He was going to break her heart if he kept it up. Hell, his own heart would suffer as it was when he broke things off but if he truly cared about her like he said he did, he'd keep in mind that her kind, the soft, sweet, feminine kind, did not marry his kind.

They'd spend the night at her place and head straight to her family's in the morning to open presents and have a big breakfast and then after some time there, head over to his family's house and do the same. It wasn't fair to her. He should have cut things off before Christmas. He shouldn't have invited her there that night but he was weak and it felt so good to have her with him.

Chapter Nine

Charity was sure she'd not be able to eat another bite but it would be mandatory to eat and eat some more at the Bettencourt's. She and Gabe had spent the first half of the day with her family and now she needed to get her butt in gear to make it over to his family's on time.

She tried not to break any laws on her way over, fudging the speed limit only a tiny bit but the tractor pulling right out into the road doing twenty miles an hour slower than she was, was more than enough to toss her plans out the window.

Worse, as she braked, debris from the tractor blew into her windshield, cracking it in a hail of rocks and dirt. Her seatbelt locked painfully across her chest as she had to brake hard without being able to see a damned thing.

"Shit!" She held on and tried to remember what she was supposed to do as her heart pounded and she got the car off to the side of the road.

With shaking hands, she managed to get her hazard lights on and out of the car. To top it all off, she had a flat tire too. Special. She called the auto club and then Gabriel to say she'd be late.

Only as she'd just connected to his cell and it started ringing, she sliced the side of her hand open as she struggled to open her trunk one handed like a dork.

He picked up right as she uttered a nasty curse.

"Hello to you too," he said, amused.

"Sorry! I'm going to be late. I'm sorry."

"Where are you? I can barely hear you. Is that traffic?"

"I had an accident and now I've sliced my hand open and I'm bleeding all over the place. I gotta go. The auto club is coming out. It'll be a while though." She hung up and began to fumble through her trunk, totally thankful when she found the box of supplies Belle had given her for her birthday, complete with a first aid kit.

She was fiddling around, ignoring her phone until she got her hand taken care of when she heard a car pull up.

"You hung up on me!" Gabriel bellowed and she started, banging her head on the open trunk in the process.

"You made me say the F word again. Why are you here and yelling at me?"

He came around the car and took her hand, slapping her other one away. "You didn't even tell me where you were. I had to guess." He hissed when he got a good look at her hand. "Christ, baby, this is a deep cut." He cleaned it out with antibacterial wash that nearly made her say the F word again and then wrapped it tight.

"I didn't hang up on you. I was bleeding all over the place. I had to get that taken care of."

He kissed her before hugging her tight. "Why did you call me *after* you called the auto club? I don't like you out here by yourself on the side of the road. Don't you know I'd help you? What the hell happened?"

She told him about the tractor and he cursed. "Damn it. He's been warned a few times. I'm going to talk to the cops about this. You could have been really hurt. As it is, you're going to have to get that crack in your windshield fixed and the tire replaced." He exhaled and visibly got himself back under control. "Are you all right?" He looked her over carefully. "Did you hit your head? You're bleeding."

He pushed her to sit on the seat of his truck.

"No, I hit my head on the trunk when you bellowed at me." She laughed. "I wasn't expecting you."

Muttering, he went to get the first aid kit. He cleaned the scratch on her scalp quickly and efficiently. "Scalp wounds bleed a lot, you know. It's not a big deal. I'll take some pain reliever when we get to your mom's house."

"I wasn't expecting you either," he said, not looking entirely pleased about it. "The auto club is here. Let me deal with them. You just sit right here."

She handed him her card and he tucked her legs into the cab and shut the door.

He managed everything and she smiled, feeling totally taken care of.

Rafe pulled up with their father and they got out.

"Oh no he did not call his family too!" she muttered as she got out of the truck, instantly sorry because the door handle hit her where she'd gashed her hand.

"I told you to stay in the truck. It's cold out here," Gabriel said as he handed her keys to Rafe. "I'm taking her to the ER to have them look at that hand. We'll be back later."

"Hello, I'm standing right here. I don't need to go to the ER. I'm fine. It's just a gash."

"You have blood all over your clothes. You're pale and your hand is bleeding again. You're going to the ER and that's final."

"Fine, then let me call my mom and have her take me. It's Christmas, Gabriel, I don't want to take you away from your family."

He sighed and looked back to his brother. "Thanks, Rafe,

Dad. Don't hold dinner for us. We'll be back as soon as we can."

Rafe chuckled and got into her car.

"Wait! Gabe's present is in the trunk."

Gabriel stomped, yes, stomped, to the trunk and pulled out a huge bag. "All this? You went a bit overboard didn't you?"

Her temples throbbed and nausea rolled through her. "No. Yours is on the top. The silver one. The rest are for your family. Have them take it all." She reached out to grab the truck and Anthony rushed to hold her up.

"Honey, sit down. Let us deal with everything."

Gabriel grunted as he picked her up like she weighed nothing and tossed her into the seat. "We can deal with presents later. You're going to the ER right now."

"This is dumb," she told him when he got into the truck and pulled back out, heading into town again. "I'm fine."

"I'm really angry right now so don't make it worse. You're pale and sweaty and bleeding. Shut up, damn it. I'm taking you and you're not going to argue."

"Pffft! I'll argue if I want. I'm just sort of shaken by the whole thing. The cut on my hand isn't even that bad and for heaven's sake, the bump on my head is just a scratch. It's Christmas, you should be with your family instead of carting me to the hospital."

"What part of *don't argue with me* did you not understand?" he grumbled but kept on driving.

Brian Taylor waited for them just inside the doors to the ER. He waved them over. "Hello there, gorgeous. Come with me, all right?" He seated her in a wheelchair while Gabriel kept close.

"Were you on duty?" Gabriel asked as Brian wheeled her around a corner and into an exam room.

"Nope. Belle called me to tell me Charity was on her way and I thought I'd pop in to check. It's pretty quiet for Christmas so you didn't pull me away from some lifesaving surgery or anything." He smiled, trying to reassure her, she knew. "Anyway, I've got hospital privileges here so why not help family out?"

"My insurance stuff is in my purse."

"I'll get it to the nurse when I go to grab a suture kit. Sit tight." He took the card and left the room.

Gabriel brushed the hair back from her face, happy to see some of her color returning and she smiled at him, apparently past her annoyance at him for taking charge.

"Okay then," Brian came back into the room, "let's get a look at you."

Just under an hour later, they left. Charity had three stitches in her hand, some butterfly bandages on the cut in her forehead and some pain relief medicine that left her sort of giddy.

No concussion or shock, thank goodness, but she was sore and she admitted she had a headache. Brian told them both to keep an eye on it and to come back if the headache didn't clear up in a few hours. Gabriel had wanted to punch that tractor driver in the damned face the whole time she had to be sewn up.

She looked over at him from her seat in his truck. "Can we stop by my house first so I can change? I hate being even more late to your family's but I'm not exactly ready for company unless it's Halloween."

"Stop worrying about being late. You know they care more about you being all right than you being there on time. And you were not *just fine*, admit it. Ms. Three-stitches-in-my-hand."

"You were right."

He laughed. "You gave me so much shit and that's all I get?"

"No. I'm perfectly willing to fix it in other ways to please you."

Her pants and sweater were covered in blood and she was paler than normal. He wanted to scoop her up and carry her off to bed while at the same time yelling at her for not calling him first. He hated the helplessness he'd felt when she'd called him and hung up without telling him where she was. Hated the punch to his gut when he saw her car there cattywompus on the side of the road and then caught sight of her hand and the blood. Most of all, he wanted to fuck her until he could sate himself of her.

"Stop that. You're hurt." God, he didn't sound the slightest bit convincing.

"Brian gave me good stuff for the pain. I'm feeling pretty darned good right now. And you look so very sexy, all gruff behind the wheel. *Grrr, don't get in my way tiny gas efficient car!*"

"I've noticed you loosen up that nice girl thing when you're tipsy," he said with a grin.

"Perfect time to take advantage, Gabriel. I'm easy and tipsy and I have to change clothes anyway. It's very economical. Also, you're a very sexed-up man and it's been about what, a whole fifteen hours since we had sex last?"

He pulled into her driveway. "You're really okay?"

She hopped out and headed to her front door. "Fine. Come on, we're late."

He followed her into the house where she waited for him to tell her what he wanted. That sweet lure of her submission wrapped around his senses, filling him up, bringing an ache only she could fill.

"Let's get you naked first and then on the bed. On your

back, I'll do all the work."

"Oh, my favorite."

She shed her clothes slowly and once they were in her room, he helped, kissing her skin as more of it was bared for him.

He froze when he saw the bruise on her shoulder near her neck.

She raised her hand to his face, moving his gaze back to hers. "Brian said the seatbelt might leave a bruise. I'm not glass, I won't break. If you can use a crop on my ass and thighs, you can make love with me right now."

Since her hand was wrapped, she couldn't really get to his buttons easily so he did it for her until they were both skin to skin.

She was so warm and alive against him he simply breathed her in for long moments before breaking away to touch more of her.

He caressed the long line of her neck, kissing over the darkness of the bruise there. "Lay back."

She got on the bed and looked up at him in that way she had. Between them there was no pretense. Nothing but them and he couldn't hide behind anything because she knew him right to his soul.

"You could have really been hurt today." He massaged up one leg and then the other, avoiding her pussy for the time being.

"I wasn't."

He smoothed over the softness of her belly, the curve of her waist, a whisper of touch over her breasts.

"We're going to be late."

He laughed. "Doesn't matter. I'm taking my time anyway."

She started to argue but he raised a brow and she

shrugged, giving in.

He kissed along the edge of her jaw, across her mouth, down her neck. She touched him with her uninjured hand, kneading his muscles, sifting through his hair. Gentle and seductive all at once.

Her nipples hardened against his tongue and she writhed a bit, gasping, when he bit just the way he knew she liked.

"God I love that. I love when you do that," she whispered as gooseflesh raised on her body beneath his lips.

He licked down her belly, delivering three sharp nips to her belly button. She widened her thighs to admit him as he moved down and set about making her feel even better.

He craved her and he knew as he moved back up to slide into her pussy that he'd never be the same. Never recover from the way he felt when he was with her.

Her legs wrapped around him, her eyes locked with his as she met his thrusts. She was the perfect everything, the perfect shape, the perfect size, smart, funny and he never wanted to let her go.

She looked up into his face. "I love you, Gabriel." It just fell from her lips, she hadn't intended to say it yet but the way he'd held her hand as he'd cleaned her wound up, the way he'd been so worried she could hear it in his voice, the way he touched her just then, all gentleness and ferocity at once—she'd been unable to hold back.

He swallowed hard and blinked as he continued to thrust into her body. "I know. I love you too. I shouldn't. We shouldn't."

"We shouldn't? Whyever not?"

"You knew what this was from the start. Just because I love you doesn't change that."

"You're seriously making this way less sexy," she grumbled and he laughed.

"Concentrate then. My cock inside you. That's what matters. You and me here right now."

She wanted to hit him. The über romantic moment of the *I love you* and he says he shouldn't love her? Total fail in the romance department.

She sighed and arched up, wanting to argue but it wasn't the time.

After the sex, which was lovely as always, even with the confession, they re-dressed and headed back out to his family's house for dinner. Still, she felt distance rather than closeness which annoyed her after the day they'd had. He'd been there for her when she needed him, darn it! He'd taken care of her, showed up, taken charge, stayed by her side through stitches and made love to her with a depth of tenderness that nearly brought her to tears. And yet he still seemed skittish.

His family had hovered around her, making sure she was well fed and comfortable even after she'd reassured them all a hundred times she was fine. There was no distance there, no skittishness, they'd taken her in completely. She was already sort of like family but now she truly had felt like one of them.

She'd been very careful with her gift to him, not wanting to spook him further. A rugged but very nice watch he could wear all day at work and it wouldn't get dinged up. His old one had stopped working just a few days before so it had been perfect timing. Other silly stuff like sweaters and a gift certificate for a massage because she thought he needed some TLC when he doled it out to everyone else all day long. He'd blushed when she said it and she'd seen the love in his eyes for her.

So why did he have to make it complicated when it was simple?

He'd given her a beautiful platinum chain, simple which

was what she preferred, but with a delicate charm, a dragonfly, one of her favorite things in the world. And cashmere gloves because her hands were always cold.

It had been very late when she finally decided to go home. She was tired and her head hurt and her heart was heavy.

She kissed Beatriz and Anthony, hugged everyone and made her way outside.

Gabriel held her good hand and opened her car door. "Are you going to sleep over?"

"I have to be up at four and you don't until eight. Go home and rest up. Get rid of that headache. I'll see you tomorrow." He kissed her so very gently.

"Thank you for today. For everything. I love you, Gabriel. If you just opened up and let this be, we could work." She didn't say anything else but got into her car and drove away.

She didn't even cry until she got into her own bed. Alone.

Chapter Ten

The day after Christmas was nearly as busy as the day before Christmas Eve. The shop was packed from the minute they opened up at nine thirty until they finally locked the doors at six.

Charity had been rushed off her feet. Too busy to leave for lunch, too busy to think on what had happened between her and Gabriel the day before. Not too busy to notice he hadn't stopped in at all, or even called, and she'd checked her phone several times just in case.

She drove home, exhausted but looking forward to a shower and hopefully some quiet time with Gabriel to work through whatever the hell was blocking him from accepting their happiness.

She left him a voicemail and jumped into the shower, careful to keep her hand dry. She took her time, letting the warmth wash away her anxiety and the stress of the day and by the time she dried off with a fluffy towel, she was smiling again.

Until she checked her voicemail.

Charity, it's me. I'm going away for a few days. I-I need to think long and hard about us. About what's going on and where this is going. I can't do that with you here, confusing the situation.

I will be back. I'm sorry if this hurts you. I do love you. God help me I do and you deserve more than a man like me. Don't you see that?

And then he'd hung up.

Oh no he did not.

She pulled clothes on as quickly as she could and rushed out to his place but it was empty. Rafe pulled his truck in behind hers before she could leave.

"Where is he, Rafe?"

He sighed. "I don't know. I really don't. I'm sorry. Honey you're going to get sick being out here with wet hair. He's just gone off to think. He'll be back."

"Well good for him. Who says I'll be waiting? Does he think he can just call all the damned shots? So I let him take over in um, well certain things, but that doesn't mean he can just walk all over me! I'm not a doormat. If he can't see what's right here in front of his eyes, he's a fool and he's right. He doesn't deserve me. Now move your truck so I can leave."

Before she could say anything else a sob escaped and Rafe was hugging her tight. "Aww, honey. I'm sorry. He doesn't think you're a doormat. No one does. He loves you. He doesn't know what to do with that. He's all hard and rough around the edges and you're so soft and pretty, he thinks that's bad for you."

"He's a halfwit. I waited for him for eight years. Eight years. I love him. He's always been inside me. But I can't do this. If he doesn't want to love me, he's right, he doesn't deserve me. I'm a good woman. I'd make a good wife for him. And that's what I want. I don't want to just be the woman he dates. I want to be his woman, his wife. I'm not willing to settle."

Rafe sighed and set her back a bit. "If I find out where he is, I'll tell you. You need to set him straight. Please don't give up on him yet."

She nodded and got into her car, waiting for him to move.

The next few days passed by in a haze. Belle came to visit several times. Marta brought over lots of movies and ice cream. Beatriz even stopped in at the shop to urge her to keep her head up and her heart open for Gabriel.

He loved her. She knew it, *she felt it.* He cared, he was gentle and thoughtful and liking it hard in the bedroom had nothing to do with that. But she'd said so and he still clung to it, so right then, things felt a bit hopeless.

In the end, she couldn't make him see it unless he wanted to. It wasn't that so very complicated and so she had to think he wanted a reason to hold back. In that case, what could she do?

She didn't just want to have great sex and this wonderfully deep connection with him if he couldn't enjoy it. She was his friend. How many people in love could say that? She *knew* him.

But if he didn't want to be known, what could she do?

Gabriel sat back at the bar and looked out over the room. He'd holed up in a hotel in Sacramento. What an idiot he was. Not a single woman in the room could hold a candle to Charity. He'd gone out to San Francisco for a few days. Toured the wine country. Went to movies. He'd even gone to a few sex shops to remind himself what he was and what she wasn't.

But he'd stood there in the aisle, staring at the toys and all he could think of was how good she'd look in the wide wrist cuffs, how she'd look with the heart imprint on her ass from the specially made paddle. And then, worse, how she'd looked each time she submitted, the way she looked up through her lashes, knowing what it did to him. That power exchange had been real. She knew what she was doing.

In short, she'd been open and loving, she'd taken all he'd offered and loved it. She'd given him her submission willingly and he'd taken it. A bond had been there already through their years of friendship and love and real love had just been waiting for the right moment.

He scrubbed his hands over his face as a woman approached. Barely dressed, too much makeup, hair overdone, drunk as hell. He sighed.

"Hi. I noticed you were alone." She dragged a chair next to him and sat, giving him quite the show in the process.

"I'm with someone." He smiled. "You're lovely and all, but I have a woman."

She leaned over him, her breasts nearly spilling from the top of the dress. He grabbed her arm to halt her progress and to keep her from falling. "Come on, tomorrow is New Year's Eve. Who's gonna kiss you when the clock strikes twelve?"

"Yes, who?"

He looked up, his heart nearly jumping from his chest at the sight of Charity there, ferociously angry, hurt and pretty scary. Her hair was loose around her face, those green eyes of hers caught the light just right and seemed to glow. Goddamn she was beautiful.

"What's it to you?" the woman trying to jump in his lap asked. Big mistake.

"What's it to me? Bitch, you best back your skanky, bare ass off. That stupid prick you're shoving your obviously fake boobs at is mine." Charity took a step forward and Gabe's cock nearly burst through his jeans. Her lush, gorgeous breasts swayed and he caught a slice of her belly where her sweater and pants met.

"Well he's not with *you* right now. He's with me."

He turned back to the woman who'd at least gotten back into her own chair. "Look, I told you..." but before he could finish the sentence Charity had tossed a drink in the woman's face.

Gabriel stood and put a hand out. The woman sputtered but stayed seated. "Baby, calm down. Nothing is going on. She threw the pitch, I didn't swing. She's drunk. Come on."

"Are you defending this skank? You want a drink in your face too?"

Wow, this was one of those unwinnable things he'd seen on television or with other men and had laughed about. He'd never seen her like this. He was sorry to have made her so upset but, and he'd never say it out loud, it was hotter than hell.

"No. I'm glad to see you. I don't want to have to bail you out of jail for a fight. Let's go and talk, okay?" He wanted to touch her but she took a step back.

"You could have seen me yesterday. Or the day before. Or the day before that. And so on. But you were obviously busy." She turned on her heel and stalked off.

He caught up with her just outside the bar. "I'm sorry. Just talk to me!"

She spun. "You, Gabriel Bettencourt, are such an asshole! I can't believe I love you. I pined for you. *Pined!* For years and years. And then in the last five days I worried about you. Worried that you'd been hurt, worried you'd think I didn't love you. And here I find you in a hotel bar with some floozy attached to you at the nipple. God!"

He took a step and kissed her, hard. Kissed her until the rigidity in her spine eased and she opened her mouth to him. Kissed her until he welcomed her taste back into his system where it belonged. Kissed her until he'd taken an edge of his jones for her and then slowly, while still holding her, pulled his mouth back.

"I'm sorry. I am an asshole. It's why I worry so much about being with you. You're so precious to me. I hate the thought of hurting you. Of disappointing you."

"So you think, hey, let's just abandon her the day after

Christmas without even an explanation." The fire was back in her eyes.

"Will you come to my room so we can talk? Please?" He held a hand out.

Charity looked at his hand, a hand he'd caressed her with, spanked her with, pulled her hair while he fucked her with, a hand he'd had on that woman's arm. Damn him.

"You think I'll just go to your room after you've been fucking other women there? I'm a nice girl but I'm not *that* nice. In fact, just thinking about what I saw when I walked into the bar makes me want to twist your balls off and feed them to feral pigs."

He winced and she sent him a grin that was as feral as she felt.

"Language, missy. I haven't been fucking anyone but you. I haven't touched, or even thought about touching any woman since you and I started up. I wouldn't do that to you. I'm a bad boy but not *that* bad. And I love you."

She tried to be unmoved by the tenderness in his touch as he slid the pad of his thumb over her bottom lip, a lip he'd only moments before had sucked in between his teeth.

"Please come talk to me."

She nodded and followed him out past the pool and to a room at the end of the wing.

No evidence of anyone else inside, and she did look. She sat in one of the chairs, trying not to look at the bed.

"How'd you find me?" he asked, picking her up like she weighed nothing and settling on the bed with her.

"You called home. Your mother called me." She shrugged and tried to move away from him but he wasn't having it. "Clearly I wasted my time."

"You didn't waste your time. I needed to think. I had to get away to do that. I did it wrong and I'm sorry for that. But I don't want you to make a mistake. I don't want to be the source of any regrets."

She struggled to free herself but he rolled them both so she ended up on her back, his body across hers.

"I don't want us running off. And I *like* the way you feel right here and right now. So tell me what you came for."

"No. You tell me what you figured out from your little vacation." It was hard not to be affected by his nearness, by the sweetness in his eyes and the "I love you" he'd given her earlier. But she needed to know what this all meant to him. She knew what it meant to her.

"You're going to make me say it first?"

"This isn't a game, Gabriel. If you don't say what I need to hear, this is over. You get your wish. I love you but I can't be with someone who doesn't want me forever."

"I hate to break it to you, baby, but you just told me what you felt."

"Seriously, this isn't cute." Although his smile made her tingly. His scent rose from the heat of his skin so very close to her mouth.

"It is. But nevermind. I'm the kind of man who likes to tie a woman's hands while he fucks her. You're this super feminine, sweet and gentle person and I suppose for the longest time, I didn't think those two things were compatible. I didn't want to sully your beauty with what I am inside."

The anguish there made her sigh. "I love what you are inside. You are never anything but gentle with me. You take care of me. You noticed my hands were always cold and you got me gloves. You knew how much I love dragonflies. You're not a bad man. You just like rough sex. It doesn't change who you are, only how you like to have sex. Those things are not mutually exclusive and I don't see why you think so. I'm not made of glass. I know what I like and I like what we do in bed. Does that make me dirty and wrong? You act like what you are is so bad, but really, good gracious, it's not *that* unusual. I like it. I consent to it. You make me happy when you're not trying to run from me."

"I'm not going to. I thought a lot about things and I'm still not good enough for you. But I don't care. I want you and I love you. You're stuck with me."

She smiled, feeling truly happy for the first time in a week. "Yeah? Not just for today or tomorrow? No more running from what we have? I need to know you're in this for the long term."

"Pushy." He grinned and kissed her quick but hard. "Long term like I want you to marry me. How's that for long term?"

"Now that's what I'm talking about."

"Good. Because I think we have time to get in the car and drive to Vegas. Come away with me and marry me tomorrow, on New Year's Eve. You'll be the one I kiss at midnight from now until forever." His expression softened.

"All right then. The store is closed until the second. I'm up for it."

Chapter Eleven

Charity looked at her hand again for the hundredth time that hour alone. Smiled when she saw the band there, marking this new step in her life but one that had been a decade in the making.

She was Charity Bettencourt now. Had been for a whole two hours. They'd driven into Vegas and to the hotel they'd been lucky to find a room at, had fabulous sex and then gone to get the license.

The best thing was that when they'd walked into the chapel just a few hours later, her parents and siblings had been there, along with his. Marta was her maid-of-honor and Rafe stood with Gabriel as his best man. It happened so fast she was glad Belle had thought to film it all so she could watch it later and get the detail lost in the haze of utter joy she'd been swamped in ever since Gabriel had proposed to her just over twenty-four hours before.

"Here, you'll need this." Gabriel handed her a glass of champagne as they looked out the windows of the club and watched the lights on the Strip just beyond.

She tiptoed up and kissed him. "Thank you."

"No. Thank you. Thank you for not giving up on me when I ran. Thank you for marrying me. I've loved you for a long time and I'll love you for the rest of my life."

"For such a dark and hard man, you sure do say some sweet stuff."

He laughed, holding her close. "It's so I can fuck you later."

"I saw the rope in the suitcase. I can't wait."

His cock pressed at her hip. His eyes darkened and his lips parted. "I can't either."

All around them, the people in the room began to count backward as midnight approached.

"Sweet, sweet Charity. Who knew good girls could be so very, very bad?"

"I've been telling you that for years now."

The clock struck midnight and his lips on hers were the best thing she'd experienced.

About the Author

To learn more about Lauren Dane, please visit www.laurendane.com. Send an email to Lauren at laurendane@laurendane.com or stop by her messageboard to join in the fun with other readers as well. http://www.laurendane.com/messageboard

Look for these titles by
Lauren Dane

Now Available:

Chase Brothers
Giving Chase
Taking Chase
Chased
Making Chase

Cascadia Wolves
Wolf Unbound
Standoff
Fated

Reading Between The Lines
To Do List
Always
Sweet Charity

Print Anthologies
Holiday Seduction

Coming Soon:

Trinity

He wasn't part of her balance sheet
But one week in his bed could tip the scales.

To Do List
© 2007 Lauren Dane

Since she could pick up a pencil, Belle Taylor has used lists and charts to map out her life. When she achieves a goal, she marks it off her to do list. Simple. But now, just steps away from her corner-office, name-on-the-letterhead goal, she realizes that the life she thought she wanted may come at too high a price.

Exhausted, she retreats home for Christmas vacation to rethink her life, complete with all-new lists. What she hadn't expected is Rafe Bettencourt, her brother's best friend, the man who she thought only saw her as a pesky younger sister. But when he kisses her under the mistletoe, Belle finds herself with a whole new set of goals to balance with what she thought she always wanted.

Rafe knows Belle is trying to figure out what to do with her life. He also knows he's done loving her from afar, and he's not beneath making it as hard as possible for her to choose to return to San Francisco.

Because Rafe can make to-do lists too—and his plan is to seduce Belle back home where she belongs. At his side. And in his bed.

Warning, this title contains the following: Smokin' hot monkey love and naughty wish fulfillment, a few words you wouldn't say in your grandma's presence.

Available now in ebook from Samhain Publishing.
Also available in the print anthology Holiday Seduction from Samhain Publishing.

He's going to give her the Christmas gift of her dreams...
in triplicate.

Unwrapped
© 2007 Jaci Burton

When Justin Garrett accidentally views Amy Parker's private online journal, he sees the cold corporate exec in a brand new light. It seems the icy, unapproachable Amy has fantasies. Fantasies that both appall and intrigue her.

No one knows the real Amy Parker, and she's satisfied to keep it that way. A woman with kinky tastes wouldn't cut it in the straight-laced law firm where she's fought her way to partnership. And she certainly refuses to let an underling use her to advance in the firm. Justin Garrett might be brilliant, gorgeous, and sexy as hell, but he's firmly restricted to her fantasies and that's where he'll stay.

While working together on a corporate acquisition in Hawaii over the Christmas holidays, Justin sets out to make Amy's secret fantasy come true—a night of passion with two men who adore her. And he knows the ideal other man to help Amy unwrap the perfect Christmas gift.

But first he has to melt her heart and convince her he sees her as a woman, not a rung to climb on the career ladder. In fact, by giving Amy exactly what she's always wished for, Justin hopes to climb right into her heart.

This title contains the following: explicit sex, graphic language, ménage a trois, a trip to Hawaii and maybe a glimpse of Santa on a surfboard.

Available now in ebook from Samhain Publishing.
Also available in the print anthology Holiday Seduction from Samhain Publishing.

GREAT CHEAP FUN

Discover eBooks!

THE FASTEST WAY TO GET THE HOTTEST NAMES

Get your favorite authors on your favorite reader, long before they're out in print! Ebooks from Samhain go wherever you go, and work with whatever you carry—Palm, PDF, Mobi, and more.

Samhain publishing ltd

WWW.SAMHAINPUBLISHING.COM